Lord Archibald Campbell

Highland dress, arms and ornament

Lord Archibald Campbell

Highland dress, arms and ornament

ISBN/EAN: 9783741174247

Manufactured in Europe, USA, Canada, Australia, Japa

Cover: Foto ©Andreas Hilbeck / pixelio.de

Manufactured and distributed by brebook publishing software
(www.brebook.com)

Lord Archibald Campbell

Highland dress, arms and ornament

HIGHLAND DRESS
ARMS AND ORNAMENT

HIGHLAND

DRESS, ARMS AND ORNAMENT

BY

LORD ARCHIBALD CAMPBELL

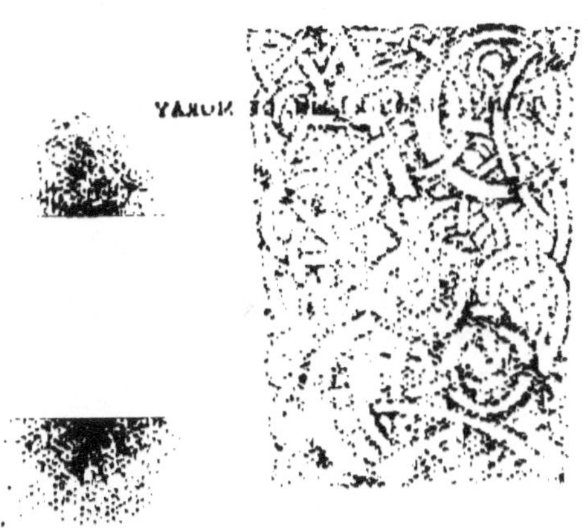

London:
ARCHIBALD CONSTABLE AND CO.
2 WHITEHALL GARDENS

Frontispiece.
JAMES, SECOND EARL OF MORAY

HIGHLAND DRESS, ARMS AND ORNAMENT

BY

LORD ARCHIBALD CAMPBELL

Westminster
ARCHIBALD CONSTABLE AND CO.
2 WHITEHALL GARDENS
1899

Of this Book 250 copies only

have been printed

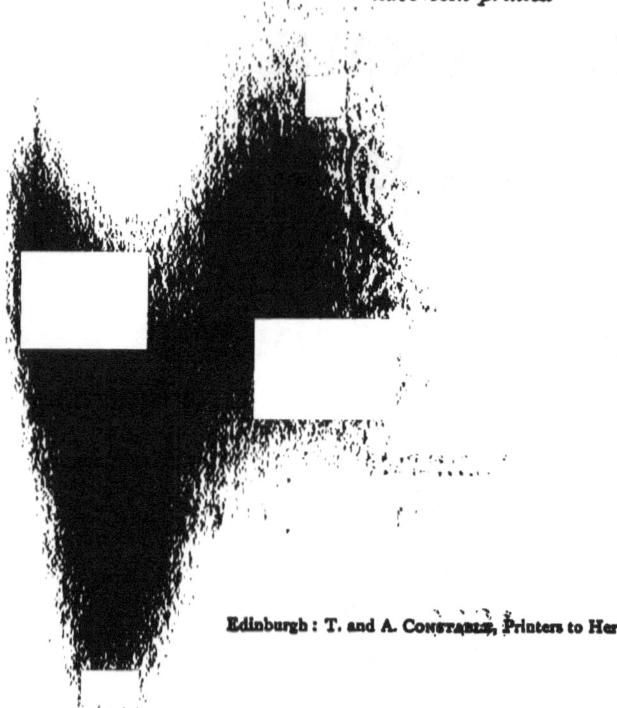

Edinburgh : T. and A. Constable, Printers to Her Majesty

596

THIS VOLUME

IS DEDICATED IN ALL LOVE TO

JOHN DOUGLAS SUTHERLAND CAMPBELL

MARQUIS OF LORNE, THE BEST AND TRUEST

OF BROTHERS, BY HIS BROTHER

ARCHIBALD CAMPBELL

The Author wishes to express his hearty thanks to Lord Edward Pelham Clinton and to numerous Friends and Correspondents for information contributed to this Work.

CONTENTS

LIST OF ILLUSTRATIONS

LIST OF BOOKS REFERRED TO

Scottish National Memorials. Published by MacLehose, Glasgow, 1890.

Swordmakers of the Middle Ages. A Lecture by Sir Henry Bessemer. Published at the Office of the *Ironmonger*, London.

Master Armourers from the Fourteenth to the Eighteenth Century. By Wendelin Boeheim. Berlin, 1897.

Ancient Scottish Weapons. Drawings by James Drummond, R.S.A. Descriptive Notes by Dr. Joseph Anderson.

Trattato Militare. By Giovan Mattheo Cigogna. 4to. Venice, 1583.

Book of True Highlanders. By C. N. MacIntyre North.

Celtic Monthly Magazine.

Book of Douglas. By Sir William Fraser.

Arsenals and Armouries in Southern Germany and Austria. By Baron de Cosson.

Notes on Swords from Culloden. By Lord Archibald Campbell. Published by C. J. Clark, 4 Lincoln's Inn Fields, 1894.

An Illustrated History of Arms and Armour, from the Earliest Period to the Present Time. By Auguste Demmin. Translated by C. C. Black, M.A.

Black Book of Taymouth.

Records of Argyll. Published by Blackwood.

Sword Belts of the Middle Ages. By Albert Hartshorne.

Sketches of the Character, Manners, and Present State of the Highlanders of Scotland. By General Stewart.

The Scottish Expedition to Norway in 1612. By Thomas Michell. Published by T. Nelson, Paternoster Row.

Les Armes. By G. R. Maurice Maindron. Paris, 1890.

Illustrated Histories of the Scottish Regiments.

Military Antiquities. Grose.

Costume. Jacquemin.

Scotland in Early Christian Times. By Dr. Joseph Anderson.

The Carved Stones of Islay. By Robert C. Graham.

Archæological Sketches in Scotland. By Captain T. P. White. MacLehose, Glasgow, 1895.

Old and Rare Scottish Tartans. By Donald William Stewart. Published by George P. Johnston, Edinburgh, 1893.

Popular Tales of the West Highlands. By J. F. Campbell of Islay.

Logan's *Gael.*

The History of the Rebellion of 1745-6. By Robert Chambers.

Waifs and Strays of Celtic Tradition.

INTRODUCTION

As a work bearing on Highland Dress pure and simple, it may be objected by some that a great deal of matter is included in this work that *per se* has nothing to do with Highland Dress. The answer is simple enough, namely, that anything worn with the Highland Dress— swords, etc., and the fashion and make of the same, necessitate allusions and quotations to the writings of many authors and to the fashions of other nations. What the Germans call a *Rundschau* or 'look round' to all countries is involved in a process of discrimination as to style and date of weapon. It is impossible to place a date on a weapon, save by contemporaneous evidence, unless evidence appear on the blade. The Highlanders did not date their work as regards sword-handle manufacture, but we are left to date weapons, roughly speaking, from family history, and from known specimens of swords yet extant.

We know that the Island of Islay contained smiths famed for the excellence of their weapons; but who has ever proved by any known mark that they could be distinctly traced to a particular year? As to this or that century the writer thinks he has adduced evidence enough for this to be done.

Of necessity these notes are but a collection of the remarks and research of many men—of men who loved swords and armour and records of dress; of others who, like Burton, had travelled much, and drew their deductions from observation of Eastern examples. He cannot, however, be reckoned as having been familiar with the weapon the Highlander used most—namely, the two-handed sword, of which he gives no example in his otherwise remarkable treatise *The Book of the Sword*. His remarks scouting the idea that the Celt was a gifted genius, and an adept in the art of beautiful and complicated ornament, do not bear close scrutiny. He imagines the beautiful scroll-work to which enthusiastic Irishmen point as evidence of a high civilisation is easily disposed of. It was all due, according to him, to the travels of the clerks and monkish artist-illuminators. But when the late Sir Richard Burton wrote thus, he little thought of the artificers and metallurgists of a far-off Celtic civilisation, or, at all events, of the beautiful specimens of Celtic patterns worked on and in metal. Penmanship is not the only proof of the art of a people. He had evidently never seen the work covering the Celtic bells, carved, as they often are, from head to foot with elaborate and exquisite patterns. This is but one instance of hasty judgment delivered by the Saxon. Look also at the jewellery of a people. Nothing can exceed the fineness of the gold and silver work of the Celtic brooch, nor can anything be more elaborate and fanciful than the lovely examples that have come down to us. Brooches made in ancient Celtic days, though similar in style, are quite peculiar, and vary in detail, and may well be called products of the genius of an artistic people. The idea that beautiful artistic work cannot come from a people inhabiting rude huts is mistaken. A modern East Indian will make a beautiful bracelet if the material be handed him, whether in a hut or by the roadside. In the same way the Celts, though they had rough surroundings, produced artistic things of the greatest beauty. These artistic instincts were transmitted to them. The bells of the Celts were of bronze and iron, and the *niello* work on them showed a very remarkable love of ornament and knowledge of metal-work. Where are the bells incrusted with these patterns elsewhere in Europe? Many bells have legends and saints and angels in 'relief' on them, and are often to be met with, but these have nothing to do with the patterns referred to.

CHAPTER I

OF SWORDS AND THEIR MANUFACTURE

THE late Sir Richard Burton, in his exhaustive work on swords, *The Book of the Sword*, has the following passage concerning the Irish and Celtic art. His remarks are found to tally with those travellers who have found the so-called Iona patterns on the shores of the Mediterranean at various places : sometimes these patterns are found in monumental stone sculptures, sometimes in illuminated MSS. :—

'The modern Irish, who in historical falsification certainly rival, if they do not excel, the Hindus, claim for their ancestry an exalted grade of culture. They found their pretensions upon illuminated manuscripts and similar works of high art; but it is far easier to account for these triumphs as the exceptional labours of students who wandered to the classic regions about the Mediterranean. If ancient Ireland ever was anything but savage, where, let us ask, are the ruins that show any sign of civilisation? a people of artists does not pig in wooden shanties, surrounded by a rude vallum of earthwork.

'Ireland, like modern Central Africa, would receive all her civilised weapons from her neighbours. The Picts of Scotland would transmit a knowledge of iron-working and of the sword to the Scotti or Picts of the north-east of Hibernia. This is made evident by the names of the articles. *Claideam* or *claidim*, the Welsh *kledyv*, is simply *gladius*; and *tuca* is *tuck*, or a clerk's sword. So *lann*, the lance-head, derives from the Gaulish spear (*lanskei*) which Diodorus Siculus terms *lagkia*, a congener of the Greek λόγχη and the Low Latin *lancea* or *lanscea*, meaning either spear (*hasta*) or sword.'

In a well-known formula, a blessing on arms and armour used in the Highlands of old before battle, 'Our broad Spanish blades' are named. We will turn to *The Book of the Sword* and see what Burton has to say as to Spanish blades. He has been treating of Italian weapons :—

'Proceeding further westward we find Diodorus Siculus (v. cap. 33) dwelling upon the Celtiberian weapons. They had two-edged swords of well-tempered steel; besides their daggers, a span long, to be used at close quarters. They made weapons and iron in an admirable manner, for they bury their plates so long underground as is necessary to eat away the weaker part; and, therefore, they use only that which is firm and strong. Swords and other weapons are made of this prepared steel; and these are so powerful in cutting, that neither shield nor helm nor bone can withstand them. Plutarch repeats this description, which embodies the still prevalent idea concerning the Damascus (Persian) scymitar and the Toledo rapier. Swedenborg introduces burial among the different methods of making steel; and Beckmann, following Thunberg, declares that the process is still used in Japan.'

Sir Henry Bessemer, in a lecture [1] delivered by him at Cutlers' Hall, gives an interesting account of the methods of the swordmaker of the Middle Ages. He says :—

'It may be instructive to pause just sufficiently to get a

---

[1] Published at the office of the *Ironmonger*, 44A Cannon Street, London.

glimpse at the system of manufacture as pursued by the artificers in steel of that period when the Bilbao, the Andrea Ferara, and the famous Toledo blades were manufactured ; for perhaps at no period of the history of steel was the skill of the workman more necessary or more conspicuously displayed. The small Catalan forges used for the production of iron and steel at that period were scattered throughout the Spanish Pyrenees and the southern provinces of France. The ores selected by the manufacturer were either the brown or red hæmatites or the rich spathose ores, still found so abundantly in Bilbao. This small blast furnace, some two feet only in height, was blown by bellows formed of the untanned skins of animals, trodden on alternately by the foot, the fuel being exclusively charcoal. It is important to remember that the ore reduced to the metallic state in the Catalan furnace never becomes sufficiently carburetted to admit of its fusion, as is the case in all the blast furnaces in use in the present day ; but, on the contrary, the metal sinks down through the burning char- coal to the lowest part of the furnace, where the lumps of reduced ore agglutinate and form an ill-shaped coherent mass, the various portions of which are more or less perfectly carburetted, so that while some portions of the lump might be classed as soft iron, other parts have passed through every grade of carburation, from the mildest to the hardest and most refractory steel. The mass of metal thus formed, and weighing from 40 lbs. to 50 lbs., is removed by simply pulling down a portion of the front of the furnace. It is then taken by the workmen to the anvil, where it is cut into smaller pieces and sorted for quality ; those portions judged by the workmen to most nearly resemble each other are put together, and, after reheating, are welded together into a rough bar. This is again cut into short lengths, which are piled together, welded and drawn out. By these successive operations the several thick lumps of which the bar was originally composed have been reduced to a number of thin layers ; and at each successive heating of the stratified mass that tendency which carbon has to equally diffuse itself results in the more highly carburised or harder portions losing some of their carbon, which is absorbed by the less carburised or milder portions of the laminated bar, thus equalising the temper of the whole mass, and conferring on it a far greater degree of uniformity in texture than at first sight would appear possible. It was clearly to the skill of the operator, and the exercise of an empirical knowledge acquired by long practice, that the world was in those days indebted for the excellent blades produced. Each piece of steel thus made had its own special degree of strength and elasticity. The artisan continually tested it again and again, and if he found it too hard he exposed the blade in the open-air for many months to rust or get milder, or he buried some parts of it in charcoal powder on his forge hearth, and patiently waited many hours while he kept up a gentle fire under it, so as to further carburise the edge or the point as he deemed advisable, but without affecting the general temper of the whole blade. He had also his own special and peculiar mode of hardening and tempering.'

2. ANDREA FERRARA SWORD, HILTED IN INDIA, AND FOUND IN THAT COUNTRY

… a texture than at first sight would appear
… quality to the skill of **the operator, and the**
… his knowledge acquired by long practice
… in those days indebted for the excellent
… Each piece of steel … had its own
… of strength and elasticity … continu-
…

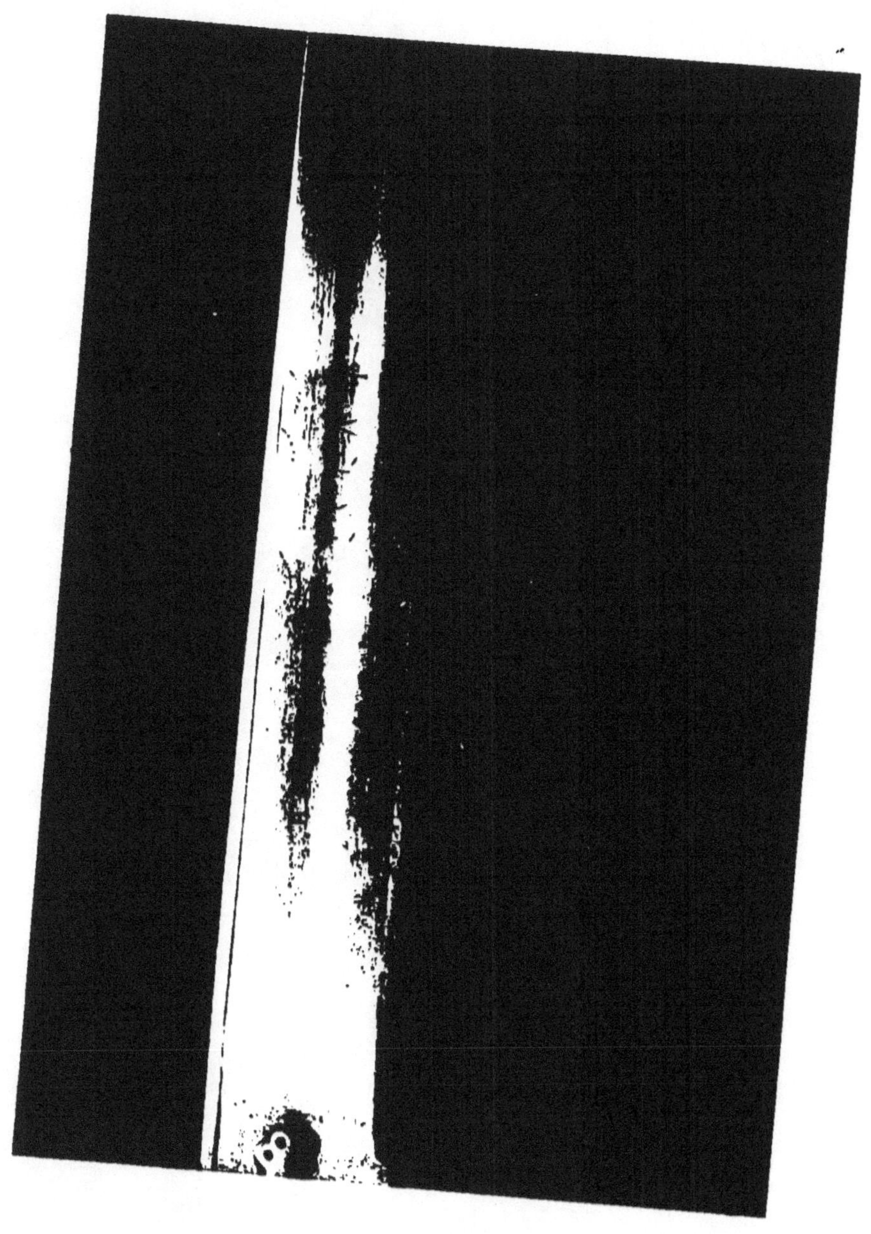

CHAPTER II

ANDREA FERRARA

WHOEVER the lucky man may be who in the future is able to 'locate' the famous armourer Andrea Ferrara, those who precede the actual discoverer may at all events be allowed to point out that the songs of the Highlanders, the blessings invoked of old, name 'Spanish' blades :—'May God bless our swords, our keen, blue Spanish blades!' (See Alexander Mac-Donald's poem of the Bìrlinn of Clanranald.)

Though it is some time since the writer met Baron de Cosson, when last speaking to him about Andrea Ferrara, he said the absence in foreign museums of the types of sword frequently to be found in Scotland was remarkable. That is to say that Andrea's weapons were manufactured for the export trade. Since seeing the Baron de Cosson, a very remarkable blade has come under the writer's notice. It had been hilted in India with a handle of Sikh type, made of iron silvered over. The whole character of the blade is most undoubtedly Spanish, as far as the writer can judge from what he has seen in Spain. A photograph

by collotype process is given of this weapon, which
has now an old Highland basket-hilt for handle.   It is
one of the very few Andreas that are really noteworthy,
of great breadth and fine temper.

In speaking of the theory that Andrea may have
worked in Spain or Portugal, a work brought out in
1890 by Messrs. MacLehose of Glasgow, called *Scottish
National Memorials*, has the following passage.   It is
headed :—

'SCOTTISH LIFE

'MILITARY

'Of the various weapons of offence which have been used in
Scotland, the two which are most distinctively national in
character are the Lochaber Axe and the Basket-hilted Sword
with Ferrara blade.   The Scottish Broadsword is distinctly
derived from the sixteenth century Schiavone of Venice ; but
what may have been the origin of Ferrara blades, and why they
became the distinctive weapons in Scotland in the seventeenth
century, are still matters of profound mystery.   In his notes to
Waverley Sir Walter Scott has the following :—

'"The name of Andrea de Ferrara is inscribed on all the
Scottish broadswords which are accounted of peculiar excellence.   Who this artist was, what were his fortunes, and
when he flourished, have hitherto defied the research of
antiquaries ; only it is generally believed that Andrea de
Ferrara was a Spanish or Italian artificer, brought over by
James IV. or V. to instruct the Scots in the manufacture of
sword-blades.   Most barbarous nations excel in the manufacture of arms ; and the Scots had attained great proficiency
in forging swords as early as the field of Pinkie, at which
period the historian Patten describes them as 'all notably

broad and thin, universally made to slice, and of such exceed-
ing good temper that I never saw any so good, so I think it
hard to devise better.'—*Account of Somerset's Expedition.* It
may be observed that the best and most genuine Andrea
Ferraras have a crown mark on the blades."

'The above note arises in connection with the expression,
"We'll put in bail, my boy; old Andrea Ferrara shall lodge
his security."—*Waverley*, chap. L.

'The legend that Ferrara was a Spanish or Italian artificer
brought over by James IV. or V., who worked his magnificent
blades in a dark Highland cave, and who killed his son for
attempting to pry into his secret of tempering steel, may at
least be dismissed; for it is obvious that, be the source what
it may, the production of Ferrara blades extended over a
period far beyond the limits of one life, and, indeed, certainly
more than one century. The name may have begun with a
single individual, and it has been pointed out that a family
of armourers bearing that name practised their art during
the 16th century in northern Italy, one of whom, said to
have been born about 1555, was named Andrea. The name,
it is certain, continued to be used largely in the manner of a
trade-mark either by persons of the Ferrara family or by
others who succeeded the original in the secrets and excellence
of his craft. An Andrea Ferrara must have been a very
common possession in Scotland during the seventeenth and
eighteenth centuries, and the number still preserved in the
country is very large. In certain rural districts, the term
"Andrea Ferrara" is to this day a recognised synonym for
sword. In this collection alone the number of Ferrara blades
shown exceeded forty, and without the least difficulty that
number might have been very largely increased. In name, and
what we may term trade or makers' marks, in the flutings
and channellings of the blades, in length and breadth, and
the whole ornamental treatment of the elaborately worked
basket-hilts, no two were alike. Mr. G. Vere Irving, F.S.A.,

in a paper descriptive of Ferrara swords, in the *Transactions of the British Archæological Association* for 1865, from twenty-five weapons described and classified fifteen varieties, in which was comprised seven variations of the spelling of the name. The most frequently recurring mark is the orb and cross ⊕┼⊷, but sometimes combined with that and sometimes separately there is a mark ⊖┼⊷. The running fox is another mark of frequent occurrence on excellent Ferrara blades, and this may be a mark imitated from the more ancient wolf blades of Passau which came to be known as foxes in England during the sixteenth century. From the works of the old dramatists it is obvious that this mark was so familiar that a sword was popularly known as a Fox. "What would you have, sister, of a fellow that knows nothing but a basket-hilt and an old fox in it?"—Ben Jonson, *Bartholomew Fair*, ii. 6. This incidental expression of the dramatist suggests that old blades may have been fitted into basket-hilts, a very probable circumstance, and one which would lead to some of the confusion which has arisen in connection with the identification of certain Scottish broadswords. While the making of Ferrara blades has not been traced to any locality in Scotland, there can be no doubt that at the time when the weapons came into common use there were armourers of sufficient skill for their fabrication in the country, as shown by the splendid pistols of Dundee, Doune, Inverness, and other places. It has been suggested that the name originated in connection with the town of Feraria in the province of Corunna in Spain, and in support of that suggestion it is pointed out that the finest existing collection of Ferrara blades is contained in the Armeria Royal of Madrid. A blade mentioned by Sir Henry Irving as being in the possession of Brodie of Brodie is marked "Andrea Ferara en Lisboa." Mr. C. N. M'Intyre North, in his *Book of the Club of True Highlanders* (vol. ii. plate xlviii.), has figured the markings on twenty-two old Scottish swords,

3. GROUP OF ANDREA FERRARA SWORDS FROM THE TWICKENHAM
SWORD RAILING

in a paper descriptive of ancient swords in the *Transactions*
of the [illegible] Archæological [illegible] for 1896, from twenty
[illegible] were examined and classified fifteen varieties in which
[illegible] seven variations of the spelling of the name. The
[illegible] early protecting mark is the orb and cross [illegible]
[illegible] overhead with that and sometimes separated
[illegible] The marking [illegible] is another
[illegible] of great occurrence on excellent Ferrara blades, and
[illegible] may be a mark imitated from [illegible] the ancient wolf
[illegible] of Passau which can [illegible] be traced [illegible] to England
[illegible] works of the old
[illegible] makes it a obvious [illegible] that
a sword was popular in [illegible]
[illegible] of a [illegible]
[illegible]

[illegible] GROUP OF ANDREA FERRARA SWORDS FROM THE TWICKENHAM
SWORD GALLERY

[illegible]
[illegible]
[illegible] decoration
[illegible] Ferrara
blade has [illegible] been traced to any [illegible] in [illegible]land, there
can be no [illegible] that at the time when the weapons came into
[illegible] as at that time were armourers of sufficient skill for their
[illegible] than in the country, as shown by the splendid sword of
Bannatyne, Doune, Inverness, and other places. It has been
suggested that the name originated in connection with the town
of Ferrara in the province of Modena in Spain [illegible] in support
of that suggestion it is pointed out that the finest existing
collection of Ferrara blades is contained in [illegible] Armeria
Royal of Madrid. A blade mentioned by [illegible] Henry [illegible]
[illegible] in the possession of [illegible]
'Andrea Ferara en Lisboa.' Mr [illegible] Smith, in
his *Book of the Club of True Highlanders* [illegible] plate XIII
has [illegible] the workings of [illegible] Scottish swords.

principally Ferrara blades. Amongst these is a claymore
preserved in Cluny Castle, on which occur the fox and the
globe marks, with a date 1414, but without any name. In
another, the property of Major Graham Stirling of Craigbarnet,
with the fox mark, the date is 1499. Mr. North also figures
three Ferrara blades in which the name occurs in conjunction
with a series of punched crowned heads, a type of which the
sword of Graham of Claverhouse, now owned by the Duke
of Montrose, is an example. There is also an excellent
blade, similarly marked, in the United Service Institution
Museum in London.'

The volume referred to was published by Messrs.
MacLehose nine years ago, and we may now be nearer
a solution of the problem of Andrea's real story
through the learned researches of Baron de Cosson.
But we never heard the Baron name the Madrid armoury
as being rich in Andreas; on the contrary, he said the
remarkable thing was the rarity of his weapons in any
of the continental armouries. This fact has been dwelt
on in a pamphlet published on the find made by the
writer of relics from Culloden, in which were very many
examples of Andrea Ferrara swords, and the name
occurred also on about forty of the small swords. There
were three channelled broadswords, two channelled
weapons, and some with a central shallow channel, all
which have been duly described, and many specimens
photographed and reproduced by collotype process, in
the said pamphlet.

In this work the matter is duly discussed, and there

can be no question that many of the specimens which went to form the famous Twickenham railing came from Solingen—and when Solingen chose, it could produce weapons of the very finest class.

When the writer, who purchased the railing, first saw it, the three sections of which it was composed were in the stable-yard at Coombe Hill Farm, whither it had been brought in a van from Richmond. One glance sufficed, notwithstanding the thick coating of green paint with which they were covered, to show that many, from their breadth, must be Highland weapons. The groove in most cases could be seen, especially when the sun was on the weapons. But the proof of this only came out under the instruments used in cleaning off the paint. For this purpose the sharpest steel scrapers made by Messrs. Holtzapffel were used. But over one hundred of the blades lay soaking in emery and oil as a preliminary step. Armour-lovers and sword-lovers will understand the pleasure derived from the cleaning process when certain famous marks appeared, such as the four crowned heads, the 'running fox,' and the older 'wolf' mark of Passau. This railing surrounded a flower-bed in the grounds of Twickenham House, and it had long been famous as being composed of weapons that were used at the Battle of Culloden. In all, 137 weapons came under the cleaning tools, and one other sword was handed in later and bought by the writer, making 138 in all. The large number of swords

4. THE ANDREA FERRARA CROWNED-HEAD
MARK FROM THE TWICKENHAM
SWORD RAILING

THE ANDREA FERRARA WOLF MARK,
FROM THE TWICKENHAM
SWORD RAILING

... can be no question that many of the specimens which ... from the ... Twickenham railway were ... Solingen steel which ... Italian ... are of ... ... very best class.

We ... the writer who purchased the railing, ... swords of which it was composed were in the ... yard at Coombe Hill Farm, whether it had been brought ... from ... One ... suffered, as with ... green paint which ... ... been.

... sword lovers will understand the pleasure derived from the ... ... upon which certain famous marks appeared, such as the four crowned scutts, the "running fox," and the other "wolf" mark ... These ... ... lower ... in the grounds of Twickenham House, and ... has long been famous as being composed of ... that were used at the ... of ... and ... ... weapons came under the ... ... and ... ... sword was ... ... and ... by ... making 138 in all. The ... ... swords ...

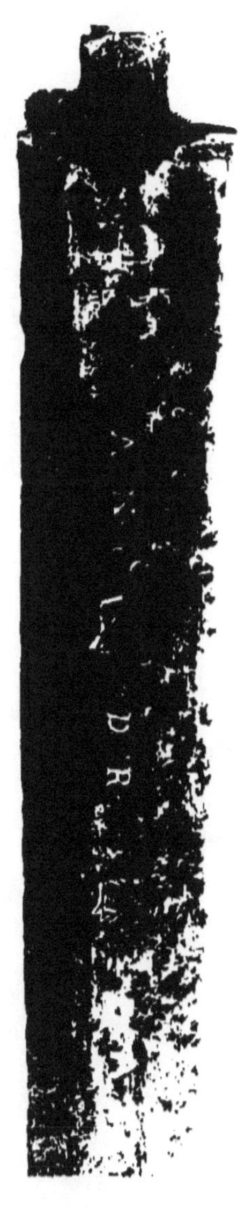

stamped Andrea Ferrara at once proved the tradition of the locality as to the origin of these weapons to have been correct, for it was in the Highland army, not in the Hanoverian army, that these weapons were carried. It would be wrong to say no Andrea Ferraras were carried by the troops of King George II., but such weapons were not a speciality or typical weapons in the Hanoverian army. Moreover, the type of many of the broadswords is purely and entirely Highland. It will be noted in another place that on the blade of the sword of Viscount Dundee, or Claverhouse, there are the four crowned kings' heads, an example of which was found in the Culloden railing.

Among antiquarians and lovers of swords Mr. G. Byng Gattie holds an honoured place. I print here some letters of his, in the first of which he refers to a pamphlet on Culloden swords written by the author of these notes, and published in 1894 by Mr. C. J. Clark, 4 Lincoln's Inn Fields.

The 'Cornhill article' to which Mr. Byng Gattie refers shall be made to follow his paper, after which follow other letters bearing on the make, the marks, and generally dealing with Andrea Ferrara swords extant.

'8th August 1894.

'MY LORD,—I have just read in the *Saturday Review* a critique on your very curious pamphlet *Notes on Swords from Culloden*. I have always felt great interest in the history of the sword—especially of the " Andrea Ferara." I beg to send you, for your courteous acceptance, a number of a Magazine containing a singular story of a genuine "Andrea Ferara" broadsword, which has been 179 years in my family (since 1715), and which, with other arms, now adorns my study here, for I value it very highly indeed.

'The gentleman mentioned under the name of "Ramsden" was my great-great-grandfather, a wealthy Lancashire squire, and the illustration is from a drawing by my wife.—I am, my Lord, yours faithfully,

'G. BYNG GATTIE,
'*Late H.M.C.S.*

'LORD ARCHIBALD CAMPBELL.

'There is an interesting history of "Andrea Ferara" in the *Cornhill Magazine*, No. 68, for August 1865.'

'*14th August* 1894.

'MY LORD,—Many thanks for your kind note, and for your appreciation of my old friend "Andrea."

'I may mention that the scabbard, in the drawing, is imaginary, the real one, silver-mounted, having been carried off, with other articles, by King George's rascally red-coated plunderers—a set of villains unworthy the name of soldiers or men.

'Should you ever be visiting this place, I should have particular pleasure in showing you my "Andrea," and another somewhat like it, which was given to me by my brother-in-law, the late Captain St. Aubyn, R.N., as a *genuine* "Andrea Ferara," but any one may see "with half an eye," from its fluted blade, etc., etc., that it is modern, though the hilt of the "four heart" pattern is very good.

'By all means, pray quote the article in the *Hour Glass*, and make any sort of reference to it you please.—I am, very faithfully yours,

'G. BYNG GATTIE,
'*Late H.M.C.S.*

'THE LORD ARCHIBALD CAMPBELL.'

5. PORTIONS OF TWO BLADES, FROM THE TWICKENHAM RAILING

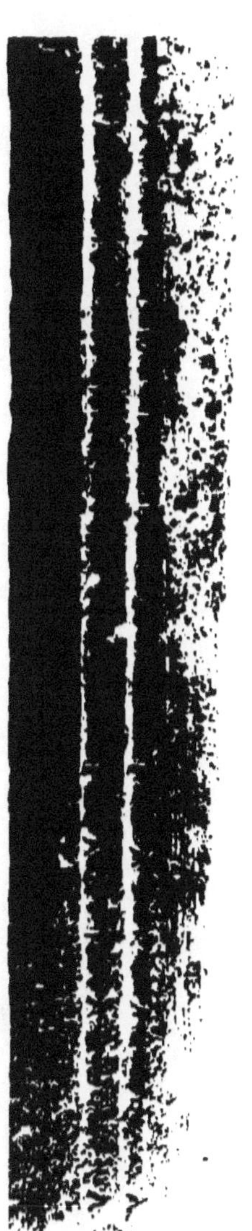

' 14th September 1894.

'MY LORD,—By this morning's post I received a copy of your pamphlet *Notes on Swords.* . . .

'I have read the work through very carefully, and with infinite pleasure, as it is a subject upon which I have always felt the deepest interest.

'I see the Baron de Cosson refers to "Ferara" by his right name of "Donato"—"Ferara," according to the affectation of the times, being merely taken from the ducal city where he appears to have had an *atelier*. But was he really *ever* in Scotland at all? Is not this a moot point? I am, yours faithfully, and much obliged,

'G. BYNG GATTIE,
' Late H.M.C.S.

'LORD ARCHIBALD CAMPBELL.'

CHAPTER III

THE STORY OF AN ANDREA FERRARA

A TRUE NARRATIVE OF 1715. IN TWO PARTS.

BY G. BYNG GATTIE.

'This sword is an " Andrea Ferara,"' said Captain Dugald Dalgetty,
'and the pistols are better than mine own.'

—*Legend of Montrose.*

PART I

'BEFORE I proceed to relate the circumstances of which the following "o'er true tale" is the narrative, it would be right and proper, perhaps, that I should say a few words, for the sole benefit of the uninitiated in such matters antiquarian, as to what is meant by an "Andrea Ferara," as set forth in the above title.

'I may therefore explain—as briefly as possible—that by an "Andrea Ferara" is simply meant a peculiar kind of basket-hilted, double-edged broadsword always held in very great esteem by the Highlanders of Scotland, into which country it was introduced sometime during the 16th century.[1] The weapon derives its name from a celebrated swordmaker whose nationality appears to be claimed by both Spain and Italy. His connection with Scotland, according to the tradition referred to by Sir Walter Scott, was brought about by the following tragical incident :—

'Andrea Ferara, described as a celebrated *Spanish* artist, had amongst his many apprentices a clever, energetic young fellow

[1] 'The basket-hilted broadswords carried by the officers of the Highland regiments of the present day are nearly identical with the "Andrea Ferara" pattern, except that the blades are not double-edged.'

6. ANDREA FERRARAS, FROM THE TWICKENHAM SWORD RAILING

CHAPTER III

THE STORY OF AN ANDREA FERRARA

(A NARRATIVE ... IN TWO PARTS)

By G. [illegible]

"This [illegible] ...
[illegible] ...

"I [illegible]

[illegible]

ANDREA FERRARA, FROM THE TWICKENHAM SWORD RAILING

[illegible]

It may therefore be [illegible] ... that
Andrea Ferrara blades ... held in such
[illegible] swords were always held in very great
esteem by the Highlanders of Scotland in which country [it]

Introduced sometime during the 16th century.[1] The
weapon derives its name from a celebrated swordsman
whose nationality appear to be claimed by both Spain and
Italy. His connection with Scotland, according to the [illegible]
referred to by Sir Walter Scott, was brought about by the
following magical incident:—

"Andrea Ferrara, described as a celebrated sword-maker, had
among his many apprentices a clever, energetic young fellow

[1] [illegible footnote]

who desired, if possible, to emulate his famous master in the manufacture of these exquisite blades.   But unfortunately, at a certain stage in the process, Ferara invariably sent away all the workmen, locked the door of the workshop, and then, by himself alone, performed some unknown operation upon the red-hot blades.   Determined to know the secret, the ambitious apprentice bored a hole in the door of the foundry, and on the very next occasion when the men were excluded he applied his eye to the aperture, and observed Ferara take a red-hot blade from the forge and sprinkle it with white powder from a sort of pepper castor.   This was immediately hammered into the hot metal, the blade returned to the furnace, and, when again heated, the same operation was repeated on the other side. This then was the great secret; although the truthful historian quite forgets to tell us whether, after all, the young man discovered of *what* the mysterious white powder really consisted.[1] However, he had discovered enough to rouse the ungovernable rage and passion of Ferara, who, on subsequently finding that he had been thus secretly watched, after bitterly upbraiding the young man for his treachery, struck him a tremendous blow on the head with the heavy hammer he held in his hand and killed him on the spot, reminding one somewhat of the well-known tale of the death of the mason's apprentice in Roslin Chapel. To avoid the consequences of this murder Ferara is said to have fled, first to France and thence to Scotland, where he was received into high favour by James V., and ultimately established a manufactory of these celebrated swords in that country.

'Such is the common tradition by which the introduction of this pattern of broadsword into Scotland is accounted for.   But

---

[1] 'It is quite possible that this "white powder" consisted of silica and alumina, which, with the carbon already in the forge, is known to produce the most beneficial effects upon steel—the prevention of rust being said to be one.   The ancient armourers of Milan and Damascus always pretended that they used diamond and ruby dust which they hammered into the red-hot steel; and it is not a little singular that Sir Isaac Newton discovered that diamonds are composed of the purest carbon, and that rubies contain silica and alumina in nearly equal parts.'

modern research has shown that there is no authority whatever for supposing that Andrea Ferara ever visited Scotland at all, far less that any of his swords were ever actually *made* there. It is quite true that his blades were greatly sought after in Scotland, but so they were in nearly every country in Europe; for it must be remembered that, in those early days, artists of great mechanical skill were few and far between, and the armourers and sword-makers of Europe were then almost exclusively confined to Spain and Italy, and there were no such cyclopean emporia as Sheffield, Birmingham, and Liége.

'The true history probably is that Andrea Ferara was born about the middle of the 16th century, and that his real name was Andrea Donato, brother of Giovanni Donato, and both connected with a large family of armourers and sword-makers who had already been known in Italy for upwards of a century. This is clearly shown by the existence, in the armouries of both Spain and Italy, of splendid blades bearing the names of Pietro Ferara, corresponding in pattern and date with those of Andrea Ferara; and others with the name of Cosmo Ferara, but evidently of a much earlier period. Their atelier was doubtless situated in the ducal city of Ferara, and the artists were commonly spoken of, according to the very affected fashion of that time, by the name of their native city, instead of their own; a custom constantly met with in the names of both painters and sculptors of the same period.

'And now, having disposed of the great swordmaker himself, I will proceed with the narrative in which one of his blades plays a somewhat interesting part.

'It was during the troublous times that preceded the landing, at Peterhead, in December 1715, of James Stuart, the son of James II., by his second wife, Mary Beatrice D'Este, that the flame of rebellion against the reigning house of Hanover was actually kindled in both England and Scotland, and great hopes were fixed on Prince James, commonly called by the English Whigs the "Young Pretender," by the English Jacobites " King James III.," by his Scottish adherents "King James VIII.," and

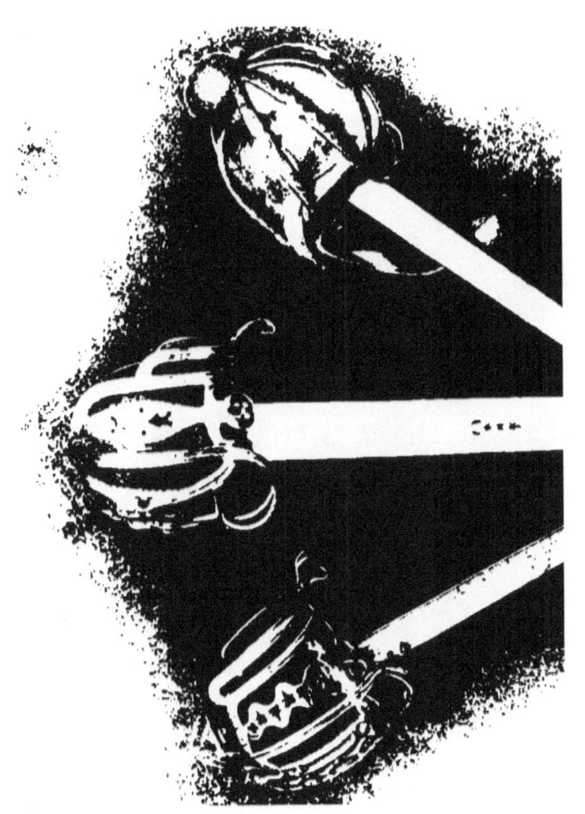

by his French friends "Le Chevalier de St. George."   James was then resident in France, buoyed up by the promises of men and money from Louis XIV. to support his claim to the throne of England, which, however, the death of that monarch put an end to, and for ever blasted all James's future chances of success.

'At this time (November 1715) the Earl of Mar, with 10,000 clansmen, held the Highlands, but was watched and overawed by the Duke of Argyll, who, at the head of the Royal troops, was strongly posted at Stirling.   The men of Northumberland had been summoned to take up arms in the Pretender's cause by the Earl of Derwentwater and by Mr. Forster, M.P. for the county.   Few, however, appear to have responded to the call of patriotism—as it was supposed to be,—and the leaders would probably have done nothing had they not been reinforced by a band of 900 Highlanders and 600 Dumfriesshire men.   Of these Mr. Forster and the Earl of Derwentwater took command, and with this handful of men had the audacity to cross the Border, and to commence hostilities.   To talk of invading a kingdom with 1500 raw undisciplined troops, commanded by wholly inexperienced leaders, seems to be about as mad and ill-judged a piece of egregious folly as could possibly be conceived ; but Forster, doubtless, counted on the populace of both countries joining his standard as he marched along—a chance that more than one invader, in former days, has been known to depend on, but generally to find himself bitterly deceived in the end.

'The invaders crossed the Border without opposition, but on reaching Penrith they were met by a force of county levies under the command of Lord Lonsdale, amounting to over 10,000 men.   It is said—however incredible it may appear—that, on catching sight of the advancing Highlanders, these brave and loyal defenders of their country turned and fled in the wildest confusion, and without even so much as firing a single shot, although they outnumbered the Scots by nearly ten to one—an exploit that certainly reflects little credit on the manhood and courage of the Cumbrians.   Continuing his

onward march, Forster was joined by about 1400 more Highlanders, under Brigadier Mackintosh, and determined at once to
advance into Lancashire with his little army of 3000 men.

'Now it so happened that two troops belonging to a regiment
of Royal dragoons were detached from the garrison of Preston,
and sent northward, during the latter part of November 1715,
under the command of Colonel Stanhope, to look out for, or at
least try and gain some intelligence of, the enemy, who was known
to have crossed the Border, and was therefore supposed to be
advancing southwards. Colonel Stanhope had already marched
many miles from Preston, and having seen nothing of the rebel
troops, appeared to have been under the impression—or to have
entertained the idea—that they were nowhere in his neighbourhood, if indeed in Lancashire at all; and subsequent events
would perhaps warrant the supposition that the Colonel had not
used during his march the care and caution so necessary with
all military operations in the face of an expected enemy.
However, be this as it may, the Colonel and his men were
slowly advancing in rather loose and careless order up a hill
and through a very open country affording little or no shelter,
and when near the summit he found himself suddenly face to
face with the advance-guard of Forster's army, consisting of a
detachment of Mackintosh's Highlanders under the Brigadier
himself. Some of these men—but by no means all—were
armed with muskets, and these were already formed so as to
present a fair front to the advancing dragoons, who had
evidently been seen by the Highlanders from this elevated
vantage-ground, and were therefore carefully waited for, with the
determination of giving his Hanoverian Majesty's troops a
reception as warm as it was utterly unexpected. Just as the
Royal dragoons reached the summit, the Highlanders—who
had been lying down—started to their feet and delivered an
irregular and an ill-directed volley almost into their faces, which,
from its very unexpected suddenness, had the effect of causing
a complete panic among the dragoons, as well as killing or

wounding one or two horses and men ; so that after a short and
. feeble show of resistance the whole squadron fairly turned
tail and galloped down the hill in the greatest confusion. Upon
seeing this the nimble-footed Scots, throwing away their useless
firelocks, now drew their trusty broadswords—their favourite
and almost national weapon—and, carrying their round targets
on their left arms, whilst the pipers struck up a soul-stirring
pibroch, with a tremendous yell they rushed like a torrent after
the retreating horsemen.

'At the foot of the hill, there stood, at that period, a handsome,
oldfashioned house built of solid stone (Steyleywood Hall),
almost surrounded by orchards and gardens, and having on one
side, a little way off, a very extensive range of stabling, barns,
outhouses and yards, which, with the adjoining estate, belonged
to a wealthy Lancashire proprietor, Ramsden by name. Into
these outhouses and yards the dragoons rode pell-mell,
determined to take advantage of whatever cover they afforded
and to make a stand against the " rebel army," as they supposed
this mere handful of Highlanders to be. Here then, amongst
the barns and outhouses, a short but desperate hand-to-hand
encounter took place ; but the majority of the dragoons contrived to get into a large barn, or granary, built of solid stone,
and closed with heavy doors, from the windows, or apertures, of
which—like a Hougomont on a small scale—they kept up such
a steady and well-directed fire with carbines and pistols at
point-blank range, that the Highlanders, having neither artillery
nor fire-arms wherewith to reply, and supposing that the Royal
army was close at hand, at once beat a hasty retreat, carrying
off their dead and wounded with them.

' As the short wintry day was now closing in, Colonel Stanhope,
leaving a sergeant's guard at the house, retired to a large
neighbouring village, where he determined to pass the night,
first sending off an express to Preston with the news of the
skirmish, and requesting to be reinforced with more troops
without a moment's delay, as the rebels were at hand.

'As soon as the soldiers were gone Mr. Ramsden took care that the guard were made thoroughly comfortable in the huge kitchen, and well supplied with substantial Lancashire fare, not forgetting plenty of good ale; and having done this, he determined to go round the outbuildings on a sort of tour of inspection in order to assure his wife and daughters—who had been nearly terrified out of their wits by the unwonted sights, sounds, noise, and confusion—that all was so far safe, and that no danger of fire anywhere existed. In this he was assisted by the bailiff and his two sons, youths of eighteen or twenty, both of whom he had, with the greatest difficulty, confined to the house during the skirmish, for they had desired to "rush into the fray," with any weapon that came handy, and so bear their part in the "battle against the rebels"—so inherent does the love of fighting and bloodshed seem to be in our common nature. One of these lads entered the army shortly afterwards and distinguished himself on more than one occasion, finally meeting a soldier's death on the field of Dettingen, in 1743, where George II. commanded in person—the last English king who ever appeared on a battlefield.

'All was found to be safe in the barns and stables ; but, in passing a cow-house, the explorers were startled on hearing a heavy groan as of some one in great agony, and on entering they discovered, by the light of their lanterns, huddled amongst some straw, a desperately-wounded Highlander. Human suffering of any kind always found ready sympathy in the large and liberal heart of Mr. Ramsden, and a cry of distress or an expression of sorrow or pain—no matter from whom—was always enough for him. At once sinking all questions of rival kings, political factions, or religious creeds, he simply saw before him a fellow-creature in a state of deplorable suffering, and instantly determined to relieve that suffering as far as lay in his power. Without word or question the wounded man was carefully raised in the powerful arms of his four Lancastrian friends, carried into the house, and laid on a bed in one of the

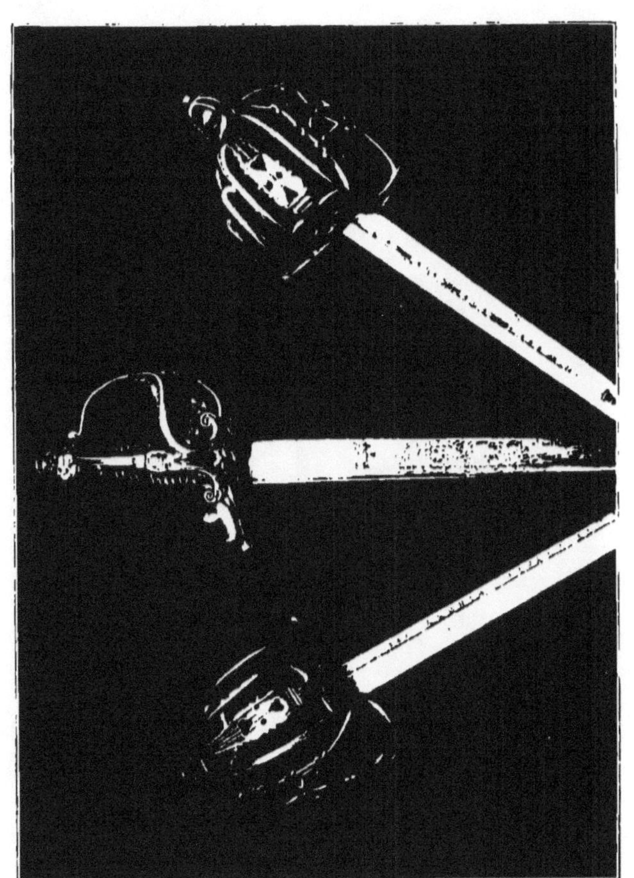

8. FROM THE QUEEN'S COLLECTION AT WINDSOR CASTLE

spare rooms. On examination he was found to have been shot through the breast, in addition to which he appeared to have received a heavy kick, as from a horse, on the right side of his head and face, which was nearly obscured by blood and dirt. Being a rebel, and actually taken with arms in his hands, Mr. Ramsden did not dare to send for medical help, and therefore he and his wife—in the broad and catholic spirit of true charity —determined to attend the sufferer themselves for the short space of time that apparently would be allotted to him in this world; for it was only too evident—even to the most un-practised eyes—that his hours were numbered, and that life, in fact, was rapidly ebbing away. On washing the mud and dirt from his face, he was found to be a remarkably good-looking young man of about twenty-four or five, possessing finely-cut aristocratic features, blue eyes, and yellow hair, "clubbed" at the back according to the military fashion of the time, but unpowdered. From the fineness of his linen, and the richness of his Highland dress and appointments, he was clearly a gentleman, probably of fortune and position, and doubtless an officer in the Pretender's army. When first discovered in the cow-house his right hand still grasped a basket-hilted broad-sword of the usual Highland pattern, but his bonnet, dirk, and target had been lost in the *mêlée*. When raised up the sword had fallen from his now powerless hand, but was picked up by one of the lads and brought into the house, and on examination it was found to be notched and bloody, showing that it had been used, and with some effect too, and that a part of the basket-hilt had been broken, probably by a shot ; but the extreme beauty and finish of the weapon, the peculiar black colouring and gilt ornaments of the basket-hilt, and the wondrous temper of the steel were at once apparent. On looking closely at the blade Mr. Ramsden—himself an excellent judge of such matters—exclaimed in unfeigned admiration, "Why, 'tis an 'Andrea Ferara,' and a genuine one, too!" and immediately deposited it in a closet close by.'

PART II

'FOR many hours, all through that weary, anxious night, the unfortunate Highlander lay in a state of perfect insensibility, but towards morning, thanks to the watchful care and skill of his friends, he opened his eyes, looked wildly round on the strange faces, but being soon assured that he was in friendly hands and had nothing to fear, he again looked eagerly round as if searching for something, and at length asked—as well as he could—for his sword, which Mr. Ramsden, with a kindly feeling for a brave man in sorrow and suffering, immediately handed to him. He received it gratefully, and laid it by him with a sort of reverence of manner. His terrible wound in the lungs, added to the fearful kick, or blow, on the side of the face, rendered speaking both painful and difficult. He, however, contrived to make Mr. Ramsden understand that he was quite aware that his end was approaching, and therefore earnestly begged that, if possible, a priest of the Roman Catholic Church might be sent for. Without a moment's hesitation, but with a high-minded disinterestedness rarely found where difference of religious opinion exists, Mr. Ramsden instantly despatched a mounted groom to the nearest town where a Roman church was established, and a priest ultimately arrived, but unfortunately not until the next morning, when his services were all but too late! The name of the sufferer was ascertained to be Mackintosh, and that he was a connection of the Brigadier. He wished, if possible, his gold watch and snuff-box to be sent to his mother in Edinburgh, together with a small miniature of a dark, foreign-looking girl which was suspended round his neck by a light blue ribbon, now, alas! no longer blue, but stained and discoloured by the life-blood of the ill-starred owner. All this, of course, Mr. Ramsden faithfully promised to do, and subsequently as faithfully carried out, and Mr. Mackintosh then

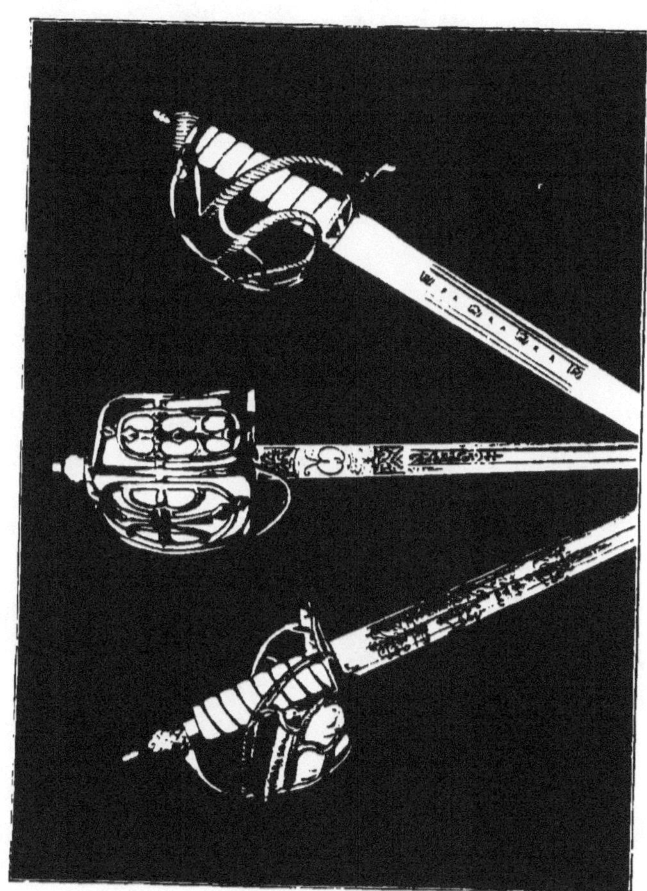

9. FROM THE QUEEN'S COLLECTION AT WINDSOR CASTLE

requested that the contents of his purse might be given to Mr. Ramsden's servants, and begged that gentleman's own special acceptance of his Highland broadsword, the history of which, with faltering breath and broken accents, and with many a pause of suffering and anguish, he, by degrees, imparted to Mr. Ramsden, and which may be condensed as follows :—

'The sword was a genuine "Andrea Ferara," and had been originally brought from Italy, many long years previously, by a relative of his family, and presented to Mr. Mackintosh's grandfather, by whom it was carried in the Scottish insurrection under Archibald, Earl of Argyll, 1685, when the owner narrowly escaped capture. It was afterwards worn by his (Mr. Mackintosh's) father in the movement in favour of James II. under James Graham, Viscount Dundee—better known as the celebrated "Claverhouse," which terminated at Killiecrankie in the death of that hero, in 1689; and, lastly, by the same gentleman at the battle of the Boyne in 1690, again fighting for James the now deposed monarch, on which occasion Mr. Mackintosh received a severe wound, of which he afterwards died. The sword at length descended to the present owner, who gloried in having been permitted to carry it, as he faintly said, "in the cause of Holy Church and of his rightful king!" A solemn pause here ensued—painful in every sense of the word to both speaker and listeners,—when, suddenly raising himself as by a desperate, but momentary, effort on his elbow, and throwing up his right arm, whilst the fire of patriotic enthusiasm lighted up his wan and haggard features, he cried, in a voice of hollow and almost supernatural tones, "God save King James the Eighth!" and instantly fell back exhausted in a swoon so completely death-like, that Mr. Ramsden quite supposed that the brave spirit had indeed taken its flight. This, however, was not the case ; the sufferer had sunk into a state of utter insensibility, from which he never awoke, and never uttered another word, during the few hours which elapsed previous to his cruel and tragical end.

'Mr. Ramsden, as already stated, was a warm-hearted, benevolent, and honourable man; but he was, at the same time, a thorough Englishman of the old Whig school, strongly attached to the cause of Protestantism, as then represented by the reigning House of Hanover, and thoroughly opposed to whatever appeared to savour of Popery in any shape or form, whether as exhibited in the Pretender himself—the son of the last Roman Catholic king of England—or in the persons of any of his friends or followers.   And he was also quite aware of the very strong feeling existing in England relative to the " Jacobite rebels," as they were commonly called, and the stringent measures adopted for their suppression, whether Scottish or English ; as well as the " no quarter " orders generally understood to have been given to the troops[1] when employed against them.   When, therefore, Mr. Ramsden, in the largeness of his true Christian heart, took in and sheltered Mr. Mackintosh, he perfectly well knew that he was incurring a very serious penalty, inasmuch as he was harbouring a rebel, actually taken red-handed, " and carrying arms against the peace of our Sovereign Lord King George the First, his crown and dignity "!   Mr. Ramsden therefore gave strict orders to the servants to keep their own counsel, and above all things to say nothing whatever about the wounded man to the sergeant or his guard, who were carousing before the kitchen fire.   But, in spite of all his caution and care, the unfortunate fact somehow leaked out—it was never known exactly *how*, but it was supposed that something must have aroused the suspicions of the sergeant, who was not only a very sharp and intelligent, but an uncommonly good-looking young man ; and he took care to make himself particularly agreeable to one of the maids, who had been repeatedly in and out of the kitchen for hot water, towels, and other appliances, and it was thought he contrived to worm the terrible

---

[1] And so fully carried out thirty years afterwards, in 1745, by ' Duke William the Butcher,' when operating against the adherents of Charles Edward, the ' Young Pretender.'

fact out of this simple Lancashire lass that a Scottish rebel was actually in the house then and there, carefully attended and assisted by the master and the inmates. However, be this as it may, it was quite certain that at daylight the sergeant sent one of his troopers to Colonel Stanhope at the neighbouring village merely to report—as he pretended—that all was quiet during the night; and it is equally certain that, at about nine o'clock in the morning, a detachment of twenty of the Royal dragoons arrived to relieve the sergeant and his guard, who thereupon immediately retired. This detachment was under the command of a certain Cornet Jobson, said to have been the son of a rich London butcher; and he most certainly carried out, in his personal appearance, and coarse, brutal manners, the attributes commonly attached to his father's trade. Forming his men before the house, he dismounted, and, taking a sergeant and six men with him, stalked up to the front door and knocked loudly. On the door being opened he pushed the footman rudely aside and walked into the house followed by the seven men, and on meeting Mr. Ramsden in the hall, replied to that gentleman's courteous salutations by saying, in a vulgar, bullying tone, that he had orders from Colonel Stanhope to search the house for concealed "Jacobite rebels"; adding, with an insolent swagger, that, as he supposed Mr. Ramsden was himself a "Jacobite," he meant to do it from "roof to cellar." Mr. Ramsden replied that so far from being a "Jacobite," he was a thorough Whig, and a loyal subject of his Majesty King George; but this was only met by a mocking, incredulous laugh, and by gestures of much impatience on the part of the soldiers, who were evidently desirous to begin their search, doubtless with a view to robbery and spoliation. Mr. Ramsden, therefore, anxious to prevent violence, at once said that he would save the cornet all further trouble, and frankly confessed that he had assisted a dying man whom he had found in a cow-shed the previous night, and who was at that moment, as he fully expected, lying dead upstairs. A grin of brutal satisfaction passed over the cornet's heavy features as he said, " Do you know you are liable to be shot for harbouring rebels ? But where is the villain ? we must have him," and forthwith ordering Mr. Ramsden, in terms far more energetic than polite, to lead the way, followed that gentleman at once to the room where the unfortunate Scot was lying. Jobson went straight up to the bed, and after attentively regarding the wounded man, and finding that he was just breathing, exclaimed with a savage laugh, turning to his men, " Ha, ha ! the rascal is still alive "—and, jerking his thumb in the direction of the bed, added, " You know your orders !" Four troopers here stepped forward to lay hold of Mackintosh, and, on Mr. Ramsden indignantly remonstrating, Jobson ordered him into custody of two of his men, who, drawing their swords, seized and held him, one on each side ; and then telling Mr. Ramsden to "interfere, at his peril, with the King's troops in the execution of their duty," bid his men " bring the prisoner out "! The four men laid violent hands on the wounded man, dragged him out of bed and, throwing a blanket over him, carried him downstairs out to the front of the house. As, of course, he could not stand, the brutal ruffians propped him up against a tree in a sitting posture, whilst a firing-party of twelve moved quickly up, and halted at ten paces. Jobson, after coolly surveying the grim preparations with that careful deliberation only acquired by much practice, at length gave the order " Fire !" and a dozen carbine bullets entered the head and body of the unfortunate young Highlander. The body, however, instead of falling over, never moved, but remained upright against the tree, and Mr. Ramsden (who had been brought down by his guards to witness the " execution ") remarked with great satisfaction that no blood whatever flowed from the many wounds, a clear proof that the poor fellow must have died whilst being dragged downstairs. Upon pointing this out to Cornet Jobson, that worthy put himself into a violent passion on having been cheated, so to speak, of his prey ; and turning to Mr. Ramsden this model "officer and gentleman" assailed

him with coarse abuse, in which the words "Jacobite, traitor, Tory, villain" were freely intermixed with oaths and imprecations; and I really believe, but for the quiet, firm representations of his sergeant, he would have ordered him (Mr. Ramsden) to have been shot on the spot. The ruffian, however, contented himself with telling him that he would be tried by court-martial, and hanged before his own door, as a traitor to his Majesty the King, and as a warning to all other such "good-natured, soft-hearted fools." Jobson then abruptly ordered Mr. Ramsden into the house, and told him to stop there, and then turning to his men appeared to be making a short speech, which they answered with a sort of cheer—apparently of approbation—for the troop immediately cantered off to the barns and stabling, which, as already stated, were situated a little way from the house. In a short time smoke was seen issuing from the outhouses and the stables, and it became evident that these redcoated scoundrels—out of sheer wanton spite and mischief—had set the whole of these buildings on fire, having first had the grace to turn out the horses, and other animals, to run loose about the land. The soldiers then formed in line between the burning buildings and the house, with their carbines full-cocked and held at the "ready," when the arch-villain Jobson roared out a warning that any one leaving the house, or attempting to check the flames, would be instantly shot. Nothing daunted, Mr. Ramsden opened the front door, and was about coming out when he was instantly fired at by Jobson himself, the bullet from his pistol striking the doorpost a few inches only from Mr. Ramsden's head.[1] It is quite probable that these scandalous proceedings might not have terminated without bloodshed, had they not been brought to a very sudden, and very unexpected, close by an express riding up in hot haste from Colonel Stanhope desiring Jobson and his men instantly to return

---

[1] The bullet was never removed, but remained sticking in the doorpost—a small but very significant monument of military cruelty and petty tyranny—until the house was taken down about the beginning of the present century.

to him, the whole detachment having received orders to repair, without an hour's delay, to Preston, as the enemy were approaching that town in force. Jobson's rage at this was great, and as he had no time to do further mischief, the miscreant had the audacity to order his men—by way of a parting salute—to fire a carbine volley into the windows of the mansion, and then, with a mocking cheer, rode off, no doubt highly satisfied with the noble courage and manly generosity he had displayed throughout this glorious morning's work, in the execution of his duty to his King and his country! As the men rode off Mr. Ramsden had the mortification to see the green velvet coat and plaid of poor Mackintosh hanging across the saddle of one of the troopers, whilst another rascal had appropriated his sword-belt, scabbard, and sporran, all mounted with massive silver, and even his shoes had not escaped the rapacity of the Royal marauders, for the sake, of course, of the rich silver buckles!

'As soon as these most unwelcome intruders had retired, Mr. Ramsden took immediate measures to have Mr. Mackintosh's body properly interred; and the funeral took place the same afternoon according to the rites of the Roman Church, the priest who had arrived in the morning officiating. Mr. Ramsden and his two sons followed, while the coffin was borne to the grave by four of his servants.

'Mr. Ramsden made repeated appeals to the Government for compensation for the heavy losses which he had sustained by the infamous outrages inflicted on his property by the ruffian Jobson, but wholly without effect, his claims being invariably met by the—unfortunately undeniable—statement that as he had thought proper to "harbour rebels" he must simply "abide by the consequences of his folly."'

L'ENVOY.

'The sword alluded to in the foregoing story is still in possession of the writer, a lineal descendant of the warm-hearted Lancashire squire referred to. It is perfectly straight, double-edged, not fluted, and of the finest steel. It has never been known to rust, a fact that would, perhaps, favour the statement that the white powder said to have been hammered into these blades was not only to strengthen the steel but to prevent oxidation. The blade is thirty-three inches long, and one and three-quarter inches broad at the hilt. The latter has been partly broken—possibly by a shot—on one side, and the whole exterior of the basket-hilt itself was apparently once covered with a kind of black Japan or enamel on which gilt flowers and ornaments seem to have been originally painted. On both sides of the blade a cross in glory is roughly represented, and below this, nearer the hilt, is cut, on a sort of fluting, in plain Roman letters, the name of the celebrated maker,

'ANDREA FARARA.'

CHAPTER IV

ANDREA FERRARA [1]—*continued*

'Sliceing swords, broad, thinne, and of an excellent temper.'[2]

'WHAT was the age and country of Andrea Ferara? This is a question which has excited and disappointed the antiquaries of Scotland and England for more than half a century. The inquiry interested Sir Walter Scott through great part of his literary life, was vainly followed by Sir Samuel Meyrick, and occupied the Deputy-Keeper of the Records in Edinburgh during a critical examination of the Chamberlain's and Treasurer's accounts, and all the documents of the Register House likely to have included the entry of payments to the celebrated swordmaker.

'These researches were undertaken in consequence of the popular belief that Andrea had visited Scotland—a supposition, however, only founded upon the number of his blades extant in this kingdom, from which it was gratuitously assumed that they had been specially manufactured for Scottish use and within the realm. Originally, however, Ferara's blades were no less common in all the Western and Southern countries of Europe, while the broadsword was a popular arm, and only in later periods became more numerous in Scotland, because this weapon was retained among the Highlanders and Borderers for more

---

[1] From the *Cornhill Magazine* for August 1865.
[2] Sir John Hayward: *Life and Raigne of King Edward the Sixth.* 4to, Lond. 1630, p. 30.

than a hundred years after it had disappeared in other nations
before the rapier and the small-sword ; but in the armouries of
Spain, Italy, and Germany, especially in the two former regions,
the number of Ferara's blades still bear witness to their ancient
prevalence.

'The belief being established that the great master had visited
Scotland, it was suggested by Sir Walter Scott that he was one
of the various foreign artificers invited by James v. to improve
the arts and manufactures of his country.[1] This supposition was
very generally received, but no evidence was discovered for its
confirmation. Meanwhile, the country of the fabricator remained
no less doubtful than his period, for, though his surname is one
of those derived from nativity or domiciliation, there are towns
of Ferara in Spain,[2] as well as the ducal metropolis in Italy ;
and thus it was uncertain in which of these cities the family of
the swordmaker had its origin. From some unknown bias, however, in Scotland, the popular belief was wholly directed to Spain,
though apparently this preference had no better foundation than
the popular intercourse of the Highlands with that country in
the sixteenth and seventeenth centuries, and the general celebrity
associated with the blades of Bilboa, Toledo, and Valencia, which
in later times had superseded the more ancient renown of the
once pre-eminent " Milan steel " ; but whatever the cause for the
nativity imputed to Ferara, a tradition current in the West
Highlands explains not only his Celtiberian origin, but the event
through which he visited Scotland.

'According to this history, Ferara was a Spanish artist, and in
the height of his celebrity had an apprentice, who was an
excellent workman, and possessed a high spirit of emulation to

---

[1] *Pitscottie Chron.* 8vo, Edin. 1814, ii. 407.

[2] In the provinces of Lerida, Coruña, and Oviedo. Madoz : *Geog. Espań.* The
name is often written indifferently, *Farrera*, *Ferraría*, and *Feraria*, but this does not
affect its identity with Farara. For the Italian city is also given as *Ferara*, *Farara*,
and *Ferare*, and all these forms are only examples of the universal uncertainty of
orthography in the middle ages, to which the name of the swordmaker was equally
subject, appearing on his blades as *Ferara*, *Ferrara*, *Farara*, and *Farrara*.

perfect his skill in the service of so great a master; his ambition, however, was disappointed by a habitude of Andrea, that when the blades were in a certain stage of forging, he excluded the workmen, and locked the door of the atelier while he performed some unknown operation, after which he again admitted the assistants to finish the blades which were in progress. The apprentice was persuaded that this seclusion concealed some occult process which essentially affected the perfection of the arms. Anxious to possess this important secret, upon the first absence of his master he bored a hole in the door of the atelier, and at the next occasion when he and his fellows were excluded returned alone to the smithy, and applying his eye to the prepared orifice, discovered his master in the act of drawing a heated blade from the forge. The lad watched with suspended breath. Ferara laid the red steel on the anvil, and taking from a bench a small tin like a flour-dredge, rapidly covered the glowing metal with a coat of white powder, which he then hammered into the iron until it was cold, when he again returned it to the fire, and having given the proper degree of heat, repeated the same operation of powdering and hammering on the other side of the blade. This process was performed in succession upon all the weapons then in progress, until, the whole being completed, Ferara laid down his hammer and turned towards the door. The varlet perceived that the mystery was at an end, and dreading to be surprised, abandoned his eyelet-hole, and fled to his companions, with whom he was immediately recalled to continue their vocations. The apprentice exulted in his discovery, but he could not boast with the ancient sage, "My secret is my own," and it escaped among his companions. These youths, being less ambitious to emulate the skill of their master than to vaunt the possession of his mystery, their disclosures were soon repeated to Ferara, and one day, when the inquisitive apprentice was alone in the smithy, Andrea entered in a tempest of wrath, and loaded him with reproaches for having betrayed the secret of his art. The young man replied with intemperance; and in the heat of their altercation Ferara struck him on the head with a hammer which he had in his hand, and laid him senseless at his feet. The blow was fatal, and to avoid pursuit for the homicide Andrea fled the country and escaped into France, from whence, in an itinerant exercise of his profession—not uncommon in the middle ages, and still continued in the *Wanderschaft* of Germany —he passed the sea into Scotland.

'Whether there is any truth in this tradition, or whether it is a passage in the life of some other eminent armourer confounded with that of Ferara, will now perhaps never be known, but in the secret operation attributed to this artist there is a singular coincidence with two practical facts—the one in the ordinary manufacture of iron, the other in the operation of the ancient sword-blades of Damascus. In the former carbon and silica are mixed with the ore in the furnace. "The carbon combines with the oxygen of the iron, and escapes in the form of carbonic acid gas, while the silica unites with the lime," which is also present in the furnace, "and forms a kind of fluid glass or scoria, which protects the iron from the action of the atmosphere."[1] In the manufacture of the Damascus scimitars, one of the operations for producing the finest blades was to sprinkle the steel while red hot with diamond and ruby dust, and to hammer the powder into the metal.[2] This process has been ridiculed by an eminent experimenter for the "ignorant" extravagance "which used" diamond-dust for carbon, and ruby for alumina or silica;[3] but Sir Isaac Newton discovered that diamond is the purest carbon, and ruby is known to combine a mixture of alumina with a large proportion of the finest silica. It is therefore probable that the operation of the Damascus smiths was founded in a sensibility of these principles, and that, far from the result of "ignorance," it was derived from that profound knowledge of chemistry in which the Saracens had

---

[1] Wilkinson's *Engines of War*, p. 224.

[2] Arabic MS. in the Rzewusky Library. By an erratum in Wilkinson's *Engines of War*, p. 211, the title of the eminent Orientalist is given as 'Rzwruzchi.'

[3] Wilkinson's *Engines of War*, p. 211.

been the masters of the Western world.   Whether, however, the
operation was efficacious or vain, is not a question here, where
we have only to consider the coincidence between the Damascus
and the reputed Spanish process.   That they were identical in
matter as in formula, may, however, be doubtful, from the im-
probability that a medium so costly as jewel-dust could have
been commanded by a trans-Pyrenean smith.   The identity of
operation, however, is unequivocal, and this community in facts is
enhanced by a community of origin in the arts of the operators ;
for all the chemistry of Spain was derived from the Moors, and
these were only the Western line of the Saracens, who were
equally the parent stock of the mediæval Syrians ; and though
the Spanish artist should not have used diamond and ruby dust,
he might—as suggested by the British critic—have substituted
the simpler elements of the same principles, carbon in the forge,
and silica and alumina in " the white powder" amalgamated on
the anvil.

'In these considerations we have received the operation
attributed to Ferara without any relation to his nationality ;
partly because the circumstantial evidence of the tradition
indicates a verity in fact—partly, that whatever the nativity of
the operator, he might at some period of his life have wrought
in the forges of Spain,[1] or, as before said, that the legend may
have originated with another master, and become associated
with Ferara by one of those various transmigrations which
sometimes confound the personages of oral record ; but whether
the story applied to Andrea or to another, we have now to
show that in the height of his profession he was established at
the town of Belluno in Friuli, an ancient duchy of Illyria, which
in 1420 was added to Venice ; and though in the succeeding
year the eastern portion was seized by Austria, the city of
Belluno and the remaining territory continued under the

---

[1] In this alternative presumption it is to be observed that the tradition defines
only the operative domiciliation, and not the nationality of Ferara ; that he was a
' Spanish *artist*,' but not that he was a *native* of Spain.

dominion of the Doges until 1797. The evidence of Ferara's domiciliation in this province is contained in a chapter upon the most renowned swordmakers of Italy in the sixteenth century—part of a once highly esteemed military treatise, published at Venice in 1585 ; and as the account illustrates the celebrity of the artist by showing the pre-eminence of the masters with whom he was associated, we shall give the text without diminution :—

' " LAME DA SPADE, STOCCHI, PVGNALI, ET ARME DA INSTARE.

' " Se la cogitatione de i luoghi et de i maestri de me discritta sin'hora sarà puntograta, et di qualchi commodità a tutti soldati, maggiormente, sarà questa ad ogni altra qualità di persone, le quali tal sorte d'armi sogliono essercitare como sono spade, spadone, stocchi, cortelazzi et mazze de cavalli, con pugnali et arme da instare d'ogni sorte che si usano. De i maestri delle quali uolendo alcuno sapere il nome tralasciendo molti, mi restringero ne i piu eccellente che ce se retrouino ; et de i luoghi et paesi lasciando adietro la grandissima Alemagna, la Francia, et nella Spagna la famoso Valenza, doue si trouano infinite arme d'ogni sorte ; uerro all' Italia, alla quale daremo con ogni ragione il pregio et uanto di quest' arte. Et primieramente diremo di Milano, cioe nel castello si lauorano perfetissimi lauori di lame da spade et pugnali, et di diuerse altre uarie sorti de lame, che sono di buone et finissime tempre. Di Brescia non mi estendero molto, ma solo toccando il nome di due fratelli, ambi maestri sopra ogn'altro eccellentissimi, i quali sono Simone et Serafino, figlioli & heredi del famoso et tanto celebrato Maestro Serafino, che faceua lame con tempre miracolose, et di esso si dice che fece una spada a un gran Principe, di tanta eccellenza, che gli dono in pagamento meglio di cinquecento ducati, oltre altre infinite marauigli che di esso si racontano. In un' altro luogo chiamato Gron su'l territorio Bergemasco, si retrouano alcuni ualenti maestri, et si chiamano quelli di Abram, che hanno bonissimo nome in quest' arte : della quale ancora perfettissimente si lauoro in Saraualle, et Ciudal de Bellun, luogi del Friuli, ne i quale si trouano ualentissime maestri d'ogni sorte ; cioe in Saraualle, Maestro Pegin da Feltran, huomo famosissimo et raro, il quale alle sue fornaci fa lauorieri miracolossi mi & in Ciudal di Bellun sono gli ingegnosi Maestro Giouan Donato et Maestro *Andrea de i Ferari*, ambidue fratelli, i quai stanno alle fusine di Messer Giouan Battista detto il Barcelone. Nel territorio Vicintino, al Monte della Madonna, a canto il fiume Reron, u'è un ualentissimo huomo detto Maestro Lorenzo da Formigano, sopranominato 'il Zotto'; questo ha buonissima fama & fa cose d'arme marauigliose di bellezza et bontà." [1]

---

[1] Giovan Mattheo Cigogna : *Trattato Militare.* 4to, Venetia, 1583, fol. 62.

'" Though the knowledge of the places and the masters described by me will be principally interesting to soldiers, it will also be acceptable to every other condition of persons who are accustomed to exercise such arms as swords, broadswords, rapiers, cutlasses, horsemen's maces, poniards, and damascined arms of all the kinds which are in use. Of those masters of whom it may be desired to know the names, omitting many in the illustrious Germany, France, and in Spain the famous Valencia, where are found numerous arms of every sort, I shall confine myself to the most excellent, with their places and countries, in Italy; to which, with every reason, we will give the pre-eminence and boast in this art. And first we will speak of Milan, where in the castle are wrought most perfect works in blades of swords, and poniards, and divers other various sorts of blades, which are of good and finest temper. Of Brescia I will not relate much, only touching the names of two brothers—both masters above all others the most excellent, and who are Simone and Serafino, sons and heirs of the so much celebrated Master Serafino who made blades of miraculous temper, and of whom it was said that he made a sword for a great Prince of such excellence, that he gave him in payment better than five hundred ducats, besides other infinite marvels which are told of him. In another place called Gron, on the territory of Bergumasco, are found some valiant masters called Abram, who have a very good name in their art, which also is wrought most perfectly in Saravalle, and in the town of Belluno, places in Friuli, in which are found excellent masters of every sort; that is, in Serravalle, Master Pegin da Feltran, a very famous and rare man, who, in his forges, makes miraculous works ! and in the town of Belluno are the ingenious Masters Giovan Donata and *Andrea of the Feraras*, both brothers, of the foundry of Master Giovan Battista, called 'the Barcelonian.' Of the territory of Vicentino, at Monte della Madonna, on the bank of the Rezon, is a most valiant man called Master Lorenzo da Formignano, called by sobriquet 'the Dolt,' who has the best fame, and makes marvellous arms for beauty and for excellence."

'The date of this notice gives an approximate indication for the period of Ferara's birth, for since he is associated with the swordmakers of the greatest celebrity in the year 1585, such eminence could scarcely have been attained under the age of thirty years; from whence it may be assumed that he was born about the year 1555. The question of his country, however, may still be liable to the cavil that as his master Giovani Battista was named "the Barcelonian," and, therefore, evidently a Spaniard, it may be conjectured that the brothers Giovan Donato and Andrea Ferara were brought by him to Italy. This supposition, however, is expressly contradicted by the author of the treatise, in the declaration that he forbore to mention the artists of

12. FROM THE QUEEN'S COLLECTION AT WINDSOR CASTLE

Germany, France, and Spain, and restricted his celebration to those of Italy alone. The notice of 'the Barcelonian' is no exception to this rule, since he is only introduced incidentally as the master of Ferara, without any reference to his own operation ; and it is not even necessarily conclusive that he was established in Italy, for, according to the prevailing usage of the mediæval craftsmen, to improve their skill in foreign schools, his pupils, Andrea and Giovani, might have resorted to Spain, to perfect their apprenticeship under a celebrated master.

'But that Ferara was a native of Italy is confirmed by the evidence that before and during his time there were others of the same surname, swordmakers in that country. This is sufficiently indicated by the mode of his denomination—"de _i_ Ferar_i_," "of _the_ Feraras," which expresses that a family of this appellation was then established, and familiarly known, if not celebrated, in the peninsula ; and that they were of native extraction is confirmed by the before-mentioned restriction of their recorder to the artists of his own country. From whence it may be concluded that the origin of the Ferari was in the ducal city of the same name. These assumptions are confirmed by the existence of blades bearing the name of Cosmo and of Piero Ferara, the last of a form coëval with those of Andrea, the first of a period about two generations anterior. The time and country of both these makers are indicated by circumstantial associations. Of Piero the nationality is presumptive in the name, which for a Spaniard had been "Pedro," while his era is evinced by the form of his blades corresponding in model with those of Andrea. In the instance of Cosmo the nationality is no less expressed by an appellation almost exclusively Italian, and the period by the form of weapons identified with the first half of the sixteenth century. This datum is confirmed by a splendid two-handed sword in our possession, bearing the distinctive features of that time, marked with the name Cosmo Ferara, accompanied by the tradition that it belonged originally to the celebrated Italian general Prospero Colonna, who died in 1523.

'From all these combinations there results a chain of circumstantial evidence, closely approaching to demonstration, that Andrea Ferara was born about the year 1555, that he was of a family of armourers which had existed in Italy at least two generations before that time, and of whom the first, like Giovani de Bologna, Leonardo da Vinci, Paolo Veronese, and a crowd of mediæval artists, derived his nomination from the place of his nativity—the ducal city of Ferara.

'Of Giovan Donato we know nothing beyond the notice of Cigogna ; but, since he is called the brother of Andrea, it is uncertain whether he was the son of the same mother and of another father, or whether the name of Donato was only a second baptismal appellation. This supposition is rendered probable from the general mediæval usage of Italy, in the popular nomination of artists by their Christian names alone, as Guido, Raphael, Claude, Salvator, Michel-Angelo, etc., an inference which is confirmed by the apparent similar example in the designation of the brother armourers Simone and Serafino, " figlioli del famoso Serafino," in which it is evident that not only the name of Simone, but that of the Serafini, father and son, was a baptismal and not a surname, for, if otherwise, the elder Serafino should have been distinguished by his prænomen. From all these considerations, therefore, it is probably conclusive that the entire name of Giovani was "Giovan Donato Ferara," and that he was full brother to Andrea.'

One of the most recent accounts of Andrea is to be found in Mr. Wendelin Boeheim's work.[1] On page 68 he says :—

'Of the two celebrated brothers the most famous was Andrea.

---

[1] *Master Armourers from the Fourteenth to the Eighteenth Century.* By Wendelin Boeheim. Berlin, 1897.

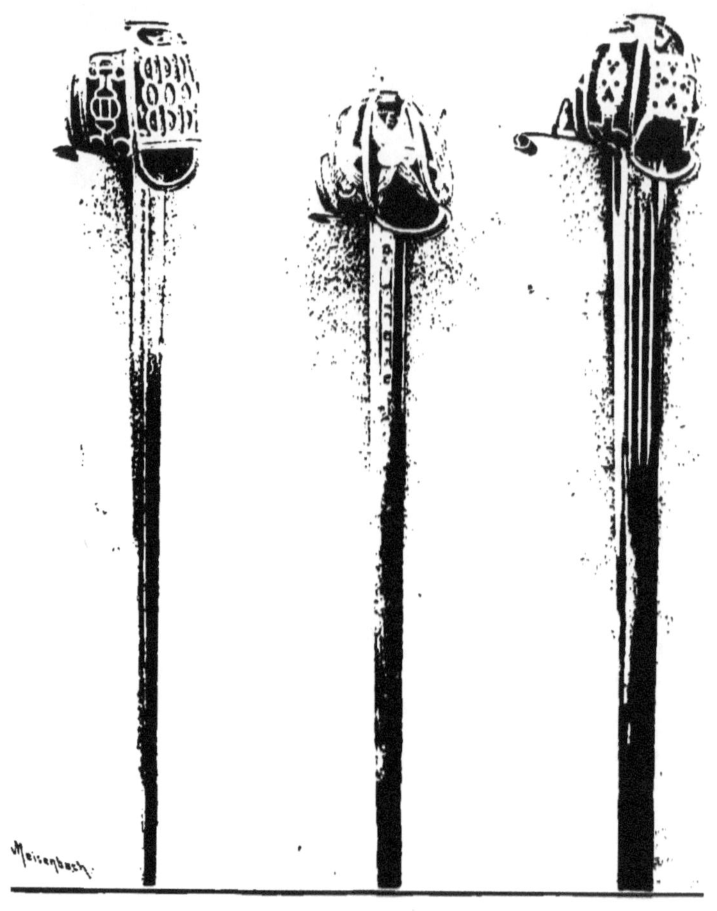

12a. SOME H
From ' Scottish

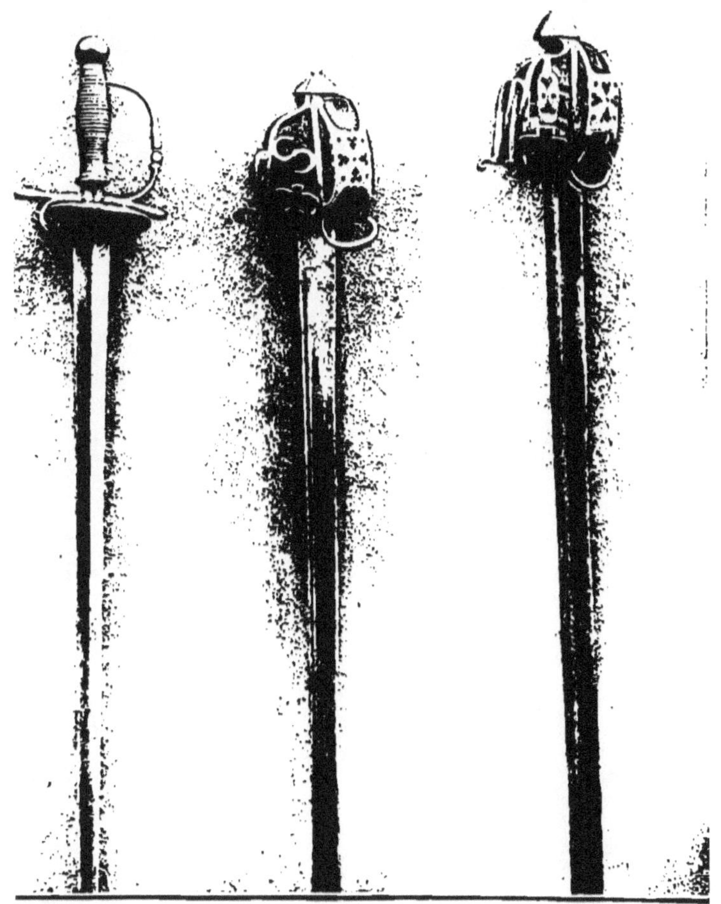

| Colonel Gardiner | Campbell of Glenlyon | Macdonald of Keppoch |
| (Prestonpans) | (Glencoe) | |

II. SWORDS

1 Memorials'

They began at first to work at Belluno, in the works of Gian-battista Barcelloni in Fisterre.

'The family bear their name, not, as asserted by Smiles and his translator, from Ferrara, but from Fonzaso. In the Records of the Cathedral of Belluno, and in the parish where the work-shops of Fisterre were, the names Ferrere, Ferraro, Ferrari, and Ferrara are often found.

'The date of the birth of the brothers Andrea and Giandonato has not come to light, but certainly show that they were at work 1567.

'According to the Register of the Parish of Cusighe, Andrea married in 1567; he must have been about thirty. Mr. Boeheim reckons we can therefore place the year of his birth as being 1530.

'In 1568 his first-born son was born, and it would appear from the Register of the Cathedral that Andrea married for a second time in 1583.

'The blades of Andrea bear his full name, frequently the letters I. H. S. beside the name: sometimes, however, they have no mark save the name.

'The names on the blades of both brothers are often found to be forgeries: carelessly read, the forgeries pass as genuine products. Forgeries were made in Seravalle and the district round.

'In Belluno it is said that Andrea brought the blades snake-shaped, or rolled snake-shaped, to the workshop,—that is to say, an imitation of the Toledo Blade manufacture.

'The year of the death of Andrea is not known.

'In Augsburg there is a large dagger in the Soeter collection manufactured by him.

'Many of his blades, though not all, carry a crowned S on a label, in imitation of the Sahagun blades.

'In the Palace of Stockholm are blades by both the brothers. (Gallery 71, 74).

'In the Imperial collection of dress at Vienna an Italian

Landsknecht's sword bears Andrea's name with a Saint Andrew's cross punctured at the extremities.

'In 1895 an Italian sword with Andrea Feraro on the blade was to be seen at an auction of the Kuppelmayer collection; above was a cross (not St. Andrew's fashion), and a snake below with open jaws.

'The Musée d'Artillerie at Paris seems to have no example of this master.

'In Venice, in the Arsenal, is a good blade by Giandonato. Another valuable example by him is in the Armoury at Gothenburg.'

Mr. Boeheim goes on to state that the blades made by Giandonato bear the name Zandona on them.

It has yet to be proved that the Venetian schiavone was the progenitor of the Highland broadsword.

A beautiful and perfect example of this weapon, the property of Mr. W. Harding Smith, was shown to the writer on March 30, 1895, by Mr. H. A. Doubleday. It bears the Venetian stamp of the Lion of St. Mark on three different places, two on the basket-guard and one on the pommel itself. A quarter of an inch from the top of the same blade is a grooved one with a back, *i.e.* a single-edged sword, and has the name Andrea Ferrara stamped on it, also the globe and cross mark.

Now, the workmanship of this sword is that of the sixteenth century. The basket-hilt, the blade, all are perfect, and very little worn.

If it can be proved that the basket-hilted broadsword of the more archaic form, several examples of which are

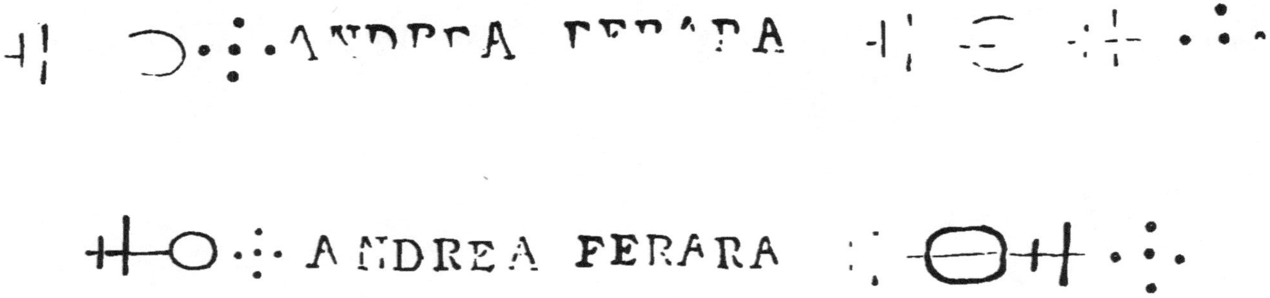

13. MARKS ON THE SWORD BELONGING TO MR. W. HARDING SMITH

shown in this work, are of earlier date than the sixteenth century, it would go far to shake the theory that the broadsword was taken from the schiavone of the Venetian Republic.

The basket-hilt of a round shape was in use in England in the reign of Henry VIII.

English writers are prone to dismiss the idea that the broadsword as used in the Highlands is of Highland or Scottish origin. But this, as everything else, has to be proved before being accepted. Germany is quite as likely as Venice to have first taken up the idea of a more rounded basket-hilt, and the types of some Scottish swords are too rough to be dismissed in a hurry. These roughly-made sword-handles are well worth studying, and date apparently further back, at all events than the schiavone shown to the writer March 30th, which is far the finest specimen that has as yet come under his notice.

There was a vast quantity of these swords for sale not long ago in Venice and elsewhere in Italy. The weapon of the common soldiers was, however, not of the same splendid quality by any means. The weapon treated of here was no doubt that of one of the officers of the Doge's guard.

Monsieur G. R. Maurice Maindron, in his work, p. 281, says that the root of schiavone is *esclavona*—sword of the slaves of the guard of the Doges. He says, further on, that in the seventeenth century the cavalry sword of the English, Italian, and German armies was moulded after this shape, while the Spanish form was that of a shell guard of various types. In this connection the following letter, which appeared in *The Times* of July 17, 1894, is interesting :—

'Your correspondent "G. A. S." is curiously incorrect, both ethnologically and historically, in what he says of the relations between Venice and the Schiavoni. It is not easy to pronounce on the derivation of the Latin word from which our "slave" is derived, but the chances are that it was borrowed from the Slavonic race, who came down into the Roman Balkans in immense numbers, and of whom many were reduced to slavery. "Slav" being probably derived from "Slava," glory, and after the manner of the Romans, it was applied to the race to which belongs the Serb, on account of their vainglorious use of the word. To this branch belonged the people of Dalmatia, Bosnia, and the Zeta, the latter being part of the family of Dushan, which always succeeded in maintaining its independence of the Turks and of Venice, while the Dalmatians became Venetian, and the Bosnians Turkish subjects. The Zeta was in close alliance with Venice, and as they held all the passes through which the Venetian overland trade with the East was carried on, they furnished the guard for the caravans. All Lower Dalmatia was then comprised in the kingdom of the Zeta, except Ragusa and those parts along the coast which had become Venetian territory; and the alliance between that kingdom and Venice lasted until the decline of the Monarchy, the last Prince marrying a noble lady of Venice, who induced him finally to take up his residence in Venice, leaving the charge of the kingdom to the Bishop, the first of a long line of Prince-Bishops, ending in the succession of the nephew of the last, Danilo, the first recognised Secular Prince of Montenegro, as the Zeta is now called by us. These Dalmatians and Montenegrins, as we may call them for the want of their old name, were all of the Orthodox faith, were a maritime people, sometimes dangerous pirates, as Venice found, and they carried on a trade with Venice, the station of which was the Riva dei Schiavoni, or quai of the Slavs or Slavons. Here the last Prince of the Zeta, about 1500, built the chapel and hospice of S. Giorgio and S. Trifonio, for the use of sailors of the Orthodox faith, now known as S. Giorgio dei Schiavoni. The Zeta furnished auxiliary troops to Venice, and were always at war with the Turks, and in the last great struggle of the Skipetar, or Albanians, under Skander Beg, the brother of the Prince fought with the Beg, and married his sister. There never was any relation between the galley-slaves and the Riva de Schiavoni, as any history of Venice will tell us. When I first went to Montenegro, there were many of the claymores to which allusion has been made offered for sale by the old Montenegrin families, in which they had been heirlooms, and I found one sculptured on a prehistoric tombstone in the far interior. It was the peculiar weapon of the Montenegrin as far back as their traditions go, and it was probably the steel derivative of the long, straight Gallic sword of which the Romans were so much afraid, till they found that they bent on thrusting, and were useless till straightened. Many of them have been found on Gallic battlefields, for "Gallic" means something different from Celtic, and probably included people of very different stocks. Be this as it may, the resemblance between the Montenegrin claymore and the Gallic sword is too striking to be left out of consideration on this subject. I have heard the Italian officers who were with the fleets at Dulcigno, and who bought all they could get, speak of the "Schiavona" as in some cases of celebrated Milanese make, and in one case at least as by Andrea Ferrara, thought by them to have been made in Milan.

'The "Stradiotti" were Skipetar, or Albanian, irregular light cavalry, and it is very doubtful if their name was derived as

"G. A. S." supposes, as they pretty certainly did not come from the Peiræus, and were only known as "Greeks" from their being of the Greek faith. I believe that the name came from their being employed as reconnoitrers or keepers of the roads (*strade*), for in the epoch of the great Venetian trade across the Balkans, being always in close alliance with the Zetans, they were probably employed in the same way. At any rate, we know nothing of them in Europe till after the defeat of Skander Beg, when thousands of them, to escape conversion to Islam, came to Italy and Sicily, where they are still considered "Greeks." The present Prime Minister of Italy is a descendant of one of these emigrants who came to Sicily. Until a late epoch they remained in the Orthodox faith. The men of the Zeta held their own in their mountains, and so did not keep company with their allies in exile, but furnished auxiliaries to Venice in Dalmatia, while the Skipetar exiles took service in Italy. They are noticed in the battle of Cadore, of which Titian painted a picture.—Yours truly,

'W. J. Stillman.

'Rome, *July* 8.'

M. Auguste Demmin says that in the Sigmaringin and Tailly collection there is a specimen of the schiavone stamped with the Winged Lion of Venice—identical, in fact, with that shown to the writer by Mr. H. A. Doubleday.

In the monumental and superb work *Ancient Scottish Weapons*, a series of drawings by the late James Drummond, R.S.A., with introduction and descriptive notes by Dr. Joseph Anderson, Keeper of the National Museum of Antiquities, Edinburgh, Plate ix., Nos. 7 and 8, show two Venetian Schiavone of the same make as the one above described, with this exception, that the pommels in both instances are nearly round in form, and are perforated with a scroll pattern. The sword belonging to Mr. W. Harding Smith has a flattened pommel, which is more often met with in the Venetian swords than the rounded perforated pattern, and is perhaps the more typical of the two.

On the same plate, No. 3, a broadsword with a broad blade, having a single channel or groove, with the name Ferrara spelt with an *e* and without the double *r*, is worth noting. It has the arc, orb, and double cross of the same pattern as the schiavone treated of at the beginning of this paragraph, but the make of the blade is different, it being very long, and double-edged.

If it is true that Andrea Ferrara worked in Lombardy, one would naturally look for specimens of his work in Venice, which lies at no great distance from the scene of his supposed manufacture.

It is worth noticing that nothing could be more utterly different in style and make than this schiavone of Mr. Harding Smith's and the finest examples belonging to the writer of broad-bladed Andrea Ferraras. Whether the spelling of Andrea Ferrara be a notable point or not, the remains of the border ornamentation, an arch with punctured dots over the same, taking the bend of the arch, is seen on some of the finest examples, and is at least worthy of note. In the case of the sword that came from India, and the termination of whose handle

is shown in one of the plates in this volume,[1] this arched
and punctured mark is continuous a good way along the
blade.   This mark is also on the Campbell of Fouachen
sword, shown at the Scottish Exhibition at the Grafton
Galleries in 1895.

[1] See Illustration at beginning of Chapter VIII.

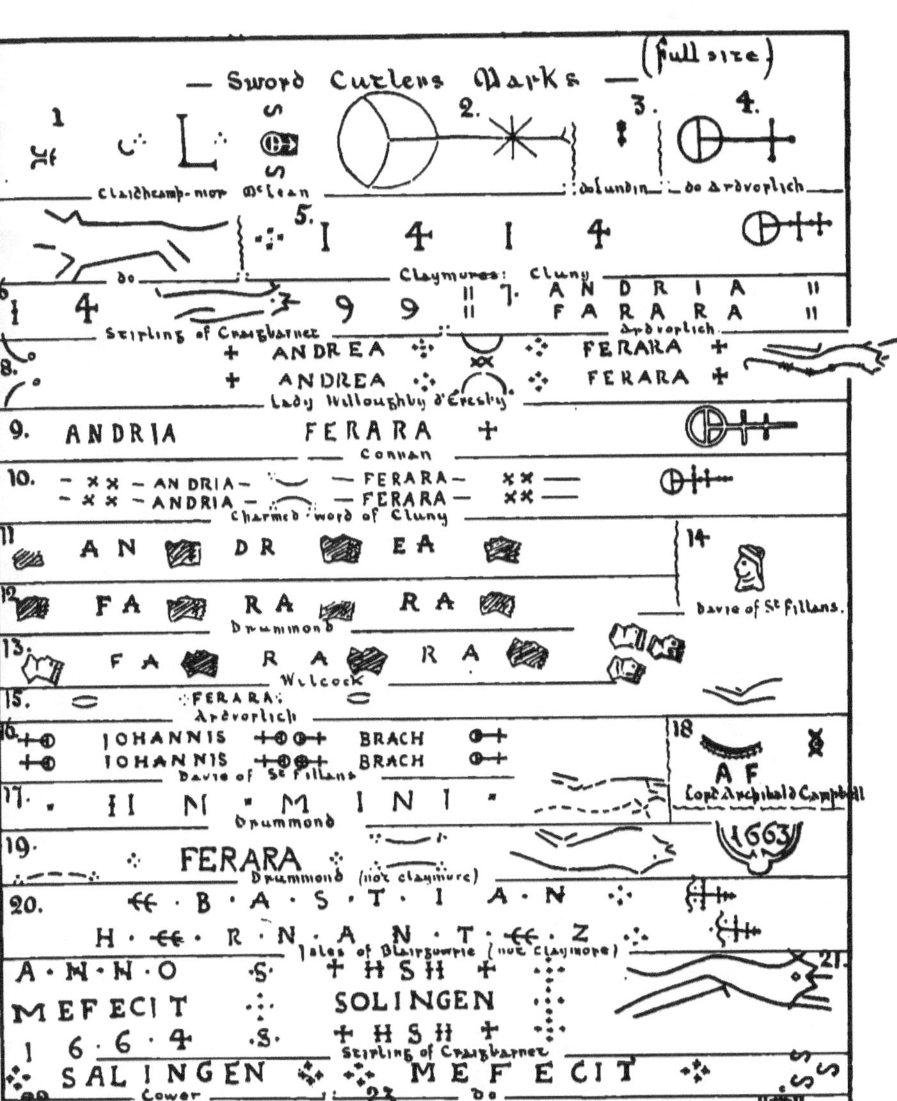

14. SWORD CUTLERS' MARKS

CHAPTER V

ON SWORD MARKS, AND SOME EXAMPLES OF SWORDS

Lovers of the sword and students of the Andrea Ferrara question must desire to fix—

1. What is the true Andrea Ferrara, or what are the true Andrea Ferrara marks? . . . In the *Book of True Highlanders*, by Mr. C. N. MacIntyre North, page 31, he has most valuable passages concerning certain well-known specimens extant in Scotland, and he comes to the conclusion that the true Andrea Ferrara blade had the following marks :—

Two punctured crosses one over the other; Andrea twice repeated, *i.e.* one over the other; and then, at equidistance from the first crosses relatively to Andrea's name, five small stars (the fifth star forming the centre). This set of stars repeated, one set being exactly above the other; then, again, two semicircles with interlaced ✕✕-shaped mark; and the five stars again repeated. Then the name Ferrara, followed by two crosses as before, one above the other; and the running wolf mark, with treble hatched cross lines on the animal's back.

Now, let us see if the ball-and-cross mark can be accepted as a test of a genuine Andrea blade.

The famous two-handed sword of MacLean of Coll, said to have been used by King Robert Bruce at Bannockburn, has the globe-and-cross mark; but in this case the cross has a St. Andrew's cross added to it; the globe also is peculiar, the intersection being a half-moon, or intersecting curve making a half-moon, to speak correctly.

The sword of Stewart of Ardvorlich has the well-known cross and globe.

The claymore belonging to Cluny, dated 1414, has four stars preceding the date, followed by a globe with a double-headed cross.

Now, if Andrea Ferrara produced a sword in 1414, and also made the sword, dated 1499, of Stirling of Craigbarnet, he must have lived and worked to a very old age.

He could not have made the sword dated 1414 before he had attained the age of fourteen, to give him the earliest possible date. This alone would put his age at ninety-nine when he produced the sword dated 1499!

We have seen elsewhere that the great armour lover and collector, Sir Noel Paton of Edinburgh, considers

the globe and cross as typical of a genuine Andrea
Ferrara, and, till a rubbing was sent to him on a sword
belonging to the writer, he was not aware of the following marks being found on a seventeenth-century sword.

This weapon may possibly have an earlier date
belonging to it; if so, it is hard to make out.   On

purchasing the weapon, the writer at once took it for
a Passau or Solingen blade.

Mr. A. Demmin gives the following account of Passau
and Solingen weapons :—

'George Springenklee, a celebrated armourer of the town of
Passau, a place famous for its arms as early as the thirteenth
century, obtained at the beginning of the fourteenth century,
from the Emperor Charles IV., armorial bearings to be used
by his township.   These arms were two crossed swords.'

Now, the sword used at Bannockburn, which was once
MacLean of Coll's property, has the globe and cross
as before stated, and the date of the battle was 1314,
so it is evident we cannot baptize all globe-and-cross
marks as being Andrea Ferrara's work and sign.   A small
globe-and-cross mark was used by a German armourer
named Johannis Brach, which sword, as delineated in
The Book of True Highlanders, belonged to Davie of
St. Fillans.

If Boeheim is correct in his statement that Andrea was

born 1530, and died 1583, a vast number of blades attributed to him must be set aside as made by far older masters of the art, or later imitators or successors to Andrea.

Decidedly it was Andrea who took the cross-and-ball mark from weapons made before Bannockburn ; and it was not his special mark only, for the weapons of Bruce's day have, at all events in one instance, a ball and cross as above mentioned.

The two-handed Highland sword used at Bannockburn by Lundie of that Ilk has a small star mark or St. Andrew's cross transfixed by a dagger-like stroke.   The two-handed sword at Cluny Castle was for two hundred years the property of the Frasers of Struie.

It will be remembered that this was the sword of the Highlanders during the wars of the Montrose period ; and that many and many a broadsword, or what is now termed claymore, was cut down in the 1745, or the earlier 1715 rising, to meet the requirements of the hour, and a handier and lighter weapon came into vogue.

Most undoubtedly one of the finest broadswords in Europe, now in the Edinburgh Museum, has the globe and cross inlaid with gold, and is a noble example of what we call an 'Andrea Ferrara.' This, with others, has been placed under glass by the able custodian, Dr. Joseph Anderson.

In the book before quoted, *Scottish National Memo-*

rials, page 105, many relics are named from the Battle of Drumclog :—

'A large drum, Andrea Ferrara sword, claymore, and Captain's sword captured at Drumclog.   Preserved by the Whytes of Neuk, Lesmahagow.   Lent by Mrs. Napier.

'Another exhibit was Andrea Ferrara broadsword from Drumclog, and the Covenanter M'Kerrow's sword, also used there.   These were lent by Mr. A. C. M'Intyre.

'Miss Julia J. Struthers lent an Andrea Ferrara broadsword used at Drumclog and Bothwell Bridge.

'Mr. Hugh Thomson showed an Andrea Ferrara rapier believed to have been used by a Covenanter at Drumclog.

'Miss Brown lent a sword used by Andrew Craig at Drumclog.

'Mr. James Fleming showed a sword used at Drumclog, and since then preserved in the family of Flemings, natives of Strathaven.

'Mrs. J. B. Dalzell exhibited the sword of a Covenanter, Muir of Darvel, used at Drumclog.   The double-edged blade is 32½ ins. long, and 1¼ ins. broad at the junction.   On each side it bears the name " Andreia Farara," and the motto " Soli Deo gloria."   It has a light basket hilt, and the grip is 3½ ins. long.

'Among other weapons shown was a brass-barrelled blunderbuss, used at Drumclog by Alexander Hetterick, and still the property of his descendant in Irvine.'

This extract is from the fine volume brought out by Messrs. MacLehose and Sons, publishers to the University, Glasgow, and is dated 1890.

The broadsword figured in *Scottish National Memorials*, page 32, is dated 1406,—that is to say, a weapon dating from the time of James I. of Scotland and of the latter days of the reign of Henry IV. of England.   The basket hilt is rough-looking, and what is called 'Early.' What evidence have we that such a form was taken from the Italian schiavone?

In Drummond's *Ancient Scottish Weapons*, plate viii. shows two examples of the Venetian schiavone, Nos. 6 and 7. No. 7 is described as being of 'Early seventeenth century.' The fine specimen shown to the writer by Mr. H. A. Doubleday was, as has elsewhere been noted, probably the sword of an officer, and had an Andrea Ferrara blade. This sword looked as if it had been made in the sixteenth century, so we see that we have yet to come across a schiavone dated before 1406; at least this must be done before we can listen to the statement that Venetians originated the basket hilt.

The present Bishop of Argyll possesses a beautiful example of a Highland broadsword, its balance when in the hand being perfect, a proof of a genuine and fine weapon. Recently, when asked some questions about it, he gave the following particulars regarding the sword :—

'1. The old sword is said to have belonged to my ancestor, Sir John Haldane of Gleneagles, who fell at the battle of Dunbar, 1650.

'2. From him it may have passed into a younger branch of the family, the Haldanes of Lanrick, to whom the late Vice-Chancellor, Sir John Stuart, was related.

'3. His son, Dugald Stuart, who married Mrs. Stuart of Dalness, showed it to me shortly before his death as the sword of my ancestor, but I forget whether he

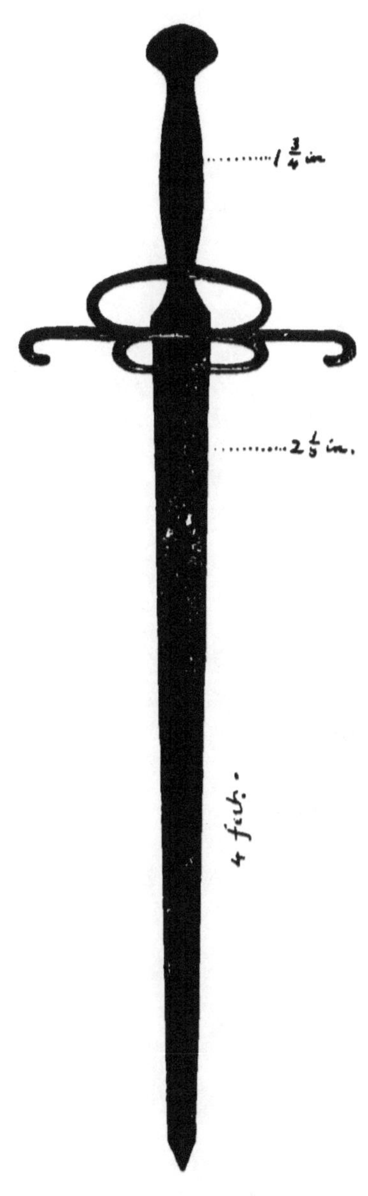

15. LIEUT.-COL. DUNCAN CAMPBELL OF
INVERNEILL'S SWORD

mentioned any name.   Mrs. Stuart of Dalness gave it me after her husband's death.

'4. It has *two* grooves.

'5. Length of the handle 5½ inches.
Length of the blade 32 inches.

'6. Width of the blade is an inch and a half near the hilt, but it tapers gradually towards the point.

'7. The *weight* of the sword is 2½ lbs. all but half an ounce.'

Lieut.-Col. Duncan Campbell of Inverneill has a very remarkable two-handed sword in his possession. The cross-guard is straight, and at each end is bent round, hook-shaped, towards the point of the weapon; the quillons, circular on the same level. The length of blade is four feet; width near the grip two inches and one-eighth; the grip or handle one foot six inches, one inch and three-quarters across the grip. The pommel is massive, of a depressed round shape. The armourer's mark is a very well-defined *fleur de lis*.

Lieut.-Col. Campbell of Inverneill thus describes the sword :—

'. . . The two-handed sword is an old family relic, and has been in our possession as chiefs of Clan Tearlach for many years. Tradition says that it was with this sword that Patrick Campbell, the then chief of the clan, killed eighteen MacGregors in a conflict near the church of Killin in 1623. He was wounded by an arrow, and died soon after; but before his death he sent his favourite gun to the head of the Craignish family as his chief. This gun was thirty inches long in the barrel, and was given by George Campbell of Craignish to his brother-in-law, Sir Duncan Campbell of Lochnell, and no doubt perished in the fire which destroyed Lochnell House fifty years ago.'

The assertion, very often made, that the S so often to be seen on the basket hilts of Scottish broadswords was a secret emblem of the Jacobites has yet to be proved.

The broadsword which belonged to Captain Campbell of Glenlyon—(it will be remembered one of Glencoe's sons was married to a niece of Glenlyon's, the sister of Rob Roy)—has a basket hilt, having the S device. Now, the sword herein referred to was lent by Colonel L. Garden Campbell at the Exhibition which took place in Glasgow, 1888.   If the theory be true that this S had to do with the Stuarts, and was emblematical of that party, all that can be said is that it must have had to do with Stuarts not of the 1715 or 1745, but of an anterior period, as the date of the massacre was 1692, and we find the type of weapon in Glenlyon's hands.

We know that vast quantities of blades were made in Germany. Whether these same basket hilts having the S simply had reference to the Scots is a question. We constantly see German blades having an inscription on them with reference to the Scotch people. They bear the legend, 'God bless the true Scots,' etc. Campbell of Glenlyon was nothing if he was not an

officer acting under orders, and he was in the service of the Protestant King.

The **S** theory is therefore rudely shaken by those who care to inquire into such matters carefully.

In the north corridor at Windsor Castle there are some two dozen superb examples of Highland broadswords, no doubt collected chiefly by the Duke of Cumberland.

The basket hilts are well-nigh all of different patterns and design. Two of them show a beautiful *fleur de lis* hand-wrought and chased, which is of greatest rarity, masterpieces of the armourer's craft.

There is also a splendid example of the four crowned kings' heads—the letters forming the name Andrea Ferrara being disposed equally between the heads, as in the sword found in the Culloden sword-railing from Twickenham House. The state of preservation of these weapons is perfect, and we must turn to the Madrid armoury to find anything to equal these examples. In one example the basket hilt is of russet and gold, and it is quite possible that such examples are of foreign manufacture; in others, a circular double ring-like mark with a central shallow hole indicates that they are of Scottish make, for this ornament exists also on numerous old examples of sporran tops.

It may be said that Germans who could manufacture splendid sword blades, imitating Italian and Spanish armourers' marks, could also easily imitate such marks on the basket hilts.   This is possible, but the Highland swords have many other peculiarities of pattern.   In the Royal collection are two fine targes of 'tough bull hide'; one of them has the fine Celtic patterns in between the large brass studs: this targe much resembles the Dunollie examples.   There are also some Highland pistols and some dirks.

The broadsword illustrated on page 32 of *Scottish National Memorials* is of importance for many reasons.

The shape and make of hilt is very early.   It is very interesting on account of its elaborately inscribed and decorated blade.

Whenever such a sword has an authenticated date, it acts as a type and lesson for all armour-lovers.

It is thus described :—

' Broadsword, with early form of basket hilt, the upper part of the blade having a shallow central channel, with both sides elaborately etched, forming a memorial of Sir John de Graham. One side bears the letters " S. J. G.," with the date 1406 in Arabic numerals, and floriated scrolls ; the other has the three scallop-shells of the Graham arms on a shield, of a form which is not earlier than the sixteenth century, and the legend—

> " Sir Jone ye Grame verry vicht and vise,
> One of ye chif reskevit Skotland thrys.
> Faucht vith yis svord and never tholit schame.
> Comandit nane to beir it bot his name." '

Sir John de Graham, the faithful ally and brother in arms of Sir William Wallace, was the second son of the knight of Dundaff in Stirlingshire, by Annabella, daughter of Robert, Earl of Strathern. He was slain at the battle of Falkirk, on 22nd July 1298, and a monument, supposed to be his, which has been several times renewed, in the churchyard there, bears an inscription, two lines of which are the same as the legend on the sword—

> 'Here lys
> Sir John the Græme baith vicht and vise,
> Ane of the chiefs reskevit Skotland thrys,
> Ane better knight not to the world was lent,
> Nor was gude Græme of truth and hardiment.'

This sword belongs to the Duke of Montrose.

On page 33 of *Scottish National Memorials* there is a description of the Douglas sword : 'The blade is double-edged, 33½ inches in length, excluding the tang, which is 6¼ inches. The blade is double-fluted on each side for a length of 10½ inches.

'In the flutings on both sides are an elaborate series of maker's marks, and between these and the tang there are later inscriptions which have been etched with acid.

'These consist on one side of the engraving of a heart, to which two hands point. Over the one hand are the letters K. R. B., and over the other the letters I. L. D.; on the other side are shown the royal shield of Scotland, with the date 1320 in Arabic numerals. The following legend is on the two sides :—

'So mony gvid as of the Dovglas beine,
Of ane svrname, wer never in Scotland seine.

I wil ye charge, efter that I depart,
To Holy gravfe, and thair bvry my hart;

Let it remane ever, bothe tyme and hovr,
To the last day I sie my Saviovr.

So I protest in tyme of al my ringe,
Ye lyk subiectis had never ony keing.

'The sword was nearly lost to the family on the occasion of the rebellion of 1745, as in their retreat from Preston the followers of Prince Charles Edward took up their quarters for a time in Douglas Castle, and carried the weapon away with them when they left. It was only after some troublesome negotiations with the rebel leaders that the sword was recovered, and replaced in the castle by the Duke of Douglas. See Sir William Fraser's *Book of Douglas*, vol. i. p. 184, where there is a coloured plate of the sword. This sword was lent for exhibition by the Earl of Home.'

In the *Celtic Monthly Magazine*, in a chapter on swords written by Mr. W. Drummond Norie, the following passage concerning the Highland sword occurs :—

'Many are the stories still extant in the Highlands of wonderful smiths who produced splendidly tempered blades

17. MACLAINE OF LOCHBUIE'S SWORD

Length of blade,	.	5 ft. 8 in.
At broadest part,	.	2½ in.
At narrowest part,	.	1¼ in.
Weight, . .	.	6 lbs. 3 oz.

without the aid of fire.   These weapons were known as "Claidheamhan fuar-iarunn," *i.e.* "cold iron swords, from the fact that they were not forged in the ordinary way, but beaten into shape by a succession of rapid blows from a heavy hammer. The celebrated hero of Glen Urquhart, au Gobha mor (the Big Smith), possessed this art, and was famed far and wide for his skill as an armourer.

'Warrior as well as smith, he performed many brave deeds with the weapons he had himself forged, and a memorial of his prowess still exists in the huge boulder known locally as Clach a' Ghobhainn Mhoir (the Big Smith's stone).   Probably he was a MacDonald, for at the present day a family of this clan living in Glen Urquhart is known as Sliochd a' Ghobhainn Mhoir (race of Big Smith).

'At Corpach, on Loch Eil, there was for some centuries a famous race of smiths whose blades were known and prized throughout the whole of the Western Highlands, and in Glen Urchay the MacNabs of Bar Chaistealan were for a period of four hundred years hereditary armourers of the Knights of Lochawe.   As late as the year 1785 a member of this family carried on the same trade, modified, of course, to suit the age in which he lived, at Baran, near Dalmally, and produced some splendid specimens of dirks, pistols, etc., some of which may still be seen in private collections of Highland arms.'

The two-handed sword, or Claidhiamh Moir, now the property of MacLaine of Lochbuie, belonged to the ancient family of Macdonell of Morar, and was carried by one of them on the occasion of the unfurling of Prince Edward Stuart's standard at Glenfinnan on the 19th August 1745.   It was borne by him both in Scotland and England while following the fortunes of the Prince, and was wielded with effect in the various battles, ending with the disastrous field of Culloden. It was afterwards carried back in safety to Dalily, on the family estate in Inverness-shire. In 1885 the sword was presented by Eneas Macdonell of Morar to Mac-Laine of Lochbuie.

The discovery of so many swords—broadswords and small-swords—bearing Andrea Ferrara's name in the Culloden fence which was at Twickenham, goes far to confirm the statements made by Baron de Cosson. He speaks again as follows in his *Arsenals and Armouries in Southern Germany and Austria* :—

'It is also certain that, common as blades bearing the signature "Andrea Ferara" are in this country, scarcely any of them are the work of Maestro Andrea de i Ferari, who gained such great renown for the superb temper of the blades which he produced in his workshop at Belluno in Venetia in the second half of the sixteenth century, where he worked with his brother Giovan Donato de i Ferari, some of whose blades, signed Laudona, still exist.

'Nearly all the blades commonly attributed to Andrea Ferara are manifestly of seventeenth-century make, and Böheim states that Andrea was born in 1530 and died about 1583. Cicogna, in his *Trattato Militare*, published at Venice 1583, specially mentions the two brothers as celebrated blade-makers.

'It is possible that a few of the finest blades existing in Scotland and England, bearing the name Andrea Ferara, may be his work, but as yet I know very few which I can positively attribute to the master, or even to the epoch when he lived, and it is curious the Italian collections possess very few even bearing his name.

'What is certain is that for nearly fifty years after his death

Solingen turned out hundreds of blades bearing his name for exportation to those countries where a true Ferara was held in high repute, just as it supplied false Toledo blades to those where a rapier was preferred to a broadsword. ' In short, it stamped Thomas Aiala on a narrow stiff blade, Sahagun on one of medium width, and Andrea Ferara on a broad flat one, as a matter of course, because each of these masters had no doubt been celebrated for that special make of blade.'

Baron de Cosson rightly notes the absence of Ferrara marked blades in Italy, where they are uncommon. But the reason for this is that the demand was very great abroad, and has continued equally so. Few Scotch or English lovers of arms would pass by an 'Andrea,' and most would reckon they had a treasure.

When the Baron wrote these lines as to Andrea's name being found on the broader character of blade, he had not been made aware that on the Culloden blades which were in the Twickenham railing Andrea's name appears on about forty small swords, also proving that Solingen accommodated all customers.

It is not impossible that some of the swords found at Culloden and placed in this railing have been adapted from sixteenth-century hilts, for they differ much in form, some having no groove at all, others having the same. It is, at all events, remarkable, and a revelation, to find Andrea Ferrara's name used on such a narrow type of sword.

It seems that prior to A.D. 1300 the quillons or cross-guards were straight; after 1350 they had curved ends (fig. 1); about 1400 they dipped (fig. 2); and in 1610 they were of the shape shown in fig. 3.

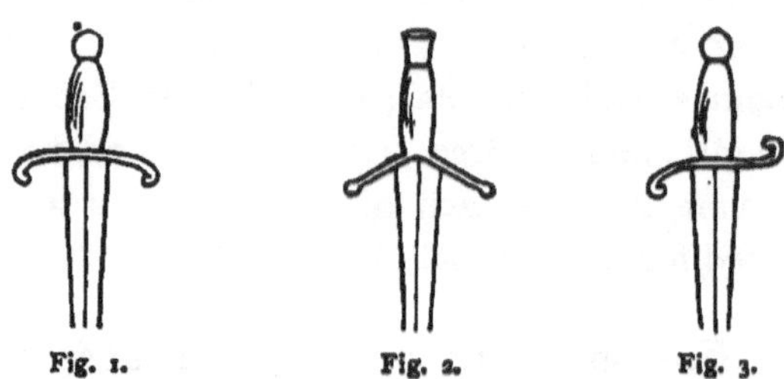

Monsieur Auguste Demmin, the author of a much-read work, *An Illustrated History of Arms and Armour, from the Earliest Period to the Present Time*, translated by C. C. Black, M.A., makes a curious mistake concerning the wearing of the broadsword. On page 371 he says :—

'The real Scottish claymore had a plain cross-guard, without the basket hilt which protected the whole of the hand : swords and sabres with these hilts are often wrongly called claymores, but they were used by the Venetians, and were called Schiavone, being the weapon used by the Doge's guards in the sixteenth and seventeenth centuries, as may be seen in pictures of that time. *In Scotland they were not known till the eighteenth century.'*

Now, when M. Demmin made this sweeping statement, he evidently was not aware of the Taymouth portrait of the second Earl of Moray. This portrait is now at Langton, Duns, N.B.[1] Moray is in full Highland dress, kilted, and has the broadsword slung

[1] Nor could he have seen the plate of the Arms of Skene, a plate of the seventeenth century.

in the ancient fashion ; the hilt of the broadsword—not the two-handed sword—is of the same pattern as many examples now shown us. It is dangerous to make such a sweeping assertion as to say they were only known in the eighteenth century when such proof to the contrary exists. It is not at all extraordinary that the weapon should have been worn earlier than the eighteenth century, when we know of plenty of examples of broadswords being in use at the time of Henry VIII. It would indeed have been strange had none of this pattern been adopted by the gentry in the North.

It is quite true that *the* sword of the Montrose wars was the true claymore, the two-handed weapon, but the other model was also known. It is strange to find so high an authority as M. Demmin wrong on such a point.

Are the types found in the Highland two-handed sword met with in other countries?

The answer to this is that the Highland weapons vary very much in the pattern of the hilts. The pommel—and there are many kinds—varies from the Norse, German, French, Italian, Swiss, and Spanish types.

The pommel is often divided into seven sections, three on either side of the central section. The ornaments at the terminations of the cross-guard are quite peculiar, ending in a punctured trefoil or quatrefoil. A glance at the swords on the tombstones, as shown in the plates, will reveal these peculiarities.

Others, again, have a round or oval pommel.   The inclination or angle of the cross-guard is very peculiar and marked in nearly all cases.

In the *Black Book of Taymouth*, Colin Campbell of Glenurchay, who died 1480, has a two-handed sword which, as he stands, touches the centre of his pauldron or shoulder-piece, coming to within an inch or two of his collar-bone.   The pommel is composed of three small globes; two below, and a central topmost ball.   The cross-guard terminates in a trefoil pierced.

The artist gives him a plaid or scarf crossing from the left shoulder, tied in a knot over the right hip, with the ends falling to very near the right knee-cap.

The next knight, Duncan Campbell of Glenurchay, killed at Flodden, 1513, is shown with a two-handed sword coming also to the centre of his pauldron.   The sword has an oval pommel surmounted with a small button, and an immensely wide cross-guard with oval terminations, not pierced but solid.

The third plate, Colin Campbell of Glenurchay, who died 1523, buried at Finlarig, shows a taller sword, with the pommel fluted into three segments, and a central button at top.   A cross-guard of solid oval terminations; a peculiar black scabbard, the chape or toe-piece broadened or flattened out.

The next knight, Duncan Campbell of Glenurchay, died 1536, aged fifty, has a sword with three flutings, a cross-guard with oval ends unpierced.

18. TWO-HANDED SWORD AT DUNROBIN
No history of Ownership.   Length 5 ft. 1½ ins.   Weight 4½ lbs.

The next knight, John Campbell of Glenurchay, who died 1550, has a sword which, as he stands, comes up to his nose; his hand is on the pommel, so that its shape cannot be seen. The cross-guards terminate in elongated, oval-shaped, solid ends, with small buttons at the apex.

The next knight is Colin Campbell, also of Glenurchay, died 1583, aged eighty-four. The pommel coming up to the mouth, as he stood, and divided into three flutings with a topmost button.

The next in order is Duncan Campbell of Glenurchay, died 1631, also buried at Finlarig, aged sixty-five. Here we see the two-handed sword for the last time in this book. The sword has a round pommel, and the cross-guard is turned up in an unusual way, curling slightly towards the grip or handle. He wears a heavy gold chain on the right shoulder.

The next knight—*ætatis suæ* 56, *anno domini* 1633—shows a sword of pure Elizabethan type, with swept quillons and cross-guard, and no longer the two-handed sword. He wears a ruff, a blue silk scarf from the right shoulder, much gold on the armour, long 'tassets' and trunk hose; his helmet plumed red, gold, and blue.

Black Duncan had an Elizabethan type of sword, as elsewhere mentioned, and not peculiarly Scottish or Highland in type. In his picture at Taymouth his arms appear in the background with the initial D-6 1601. The sword may be reckoned of the Spanish type—such a blade as was prized by Highlanders. This is proved by the words of a prayer in which special mention is made of 'our keen Spanish blades.' Vide *Records of Argyll.*

Mention has been made of, and notice drawn to, the peculiar patterns and shapes of the sword pommels of the Highland two-handed swords—namely, that they are usually divided into segments, the broadest part of the cushion-like segments being at the top, and all narrowing to an apex at the junction with the blade—the scallop-shell pattern, it may be called.

Let us see if anything like this can be traced in the South.

In a book of twenty-three pages, full of valuable information, by Mr. Albert Hartshorne, *The Sword Belts of the Middle Ages*, in the second folding plate which he gives of sword belts, No. 13 will be found to have a peculiar one, and the sword itself has a pommel divided into six sections. No. 14 has a sword attached by a perfectly plain belt, the pommel of which is divided into three sections of somewhat similar pattern. The sword first named is that of Gilbert Marshall, Earl of Pembroke, who died 1241. The other example, No. 14, is that 'from the long posthumous and excellent wooden figure of Robert, Duke of Normandy.' In another plate, a good bit further on, No. 63 has a pommel divided into three sections, with a smaller button at the top. When mention is made of the number of these examples alone in this particular work bearing real likeness to the

Scottish pattern, the idea or plan is somewhat similar, that is all that can be said. 'No. 63, from a brass of Simon Norwich, Brampton, by Dingley, Northamptonshire, is an early example of the fluted pommel and the fringed grip.' Mr. Hartshorne does not give the date; but he is speaking of examples 1465-1484, so it is presumed the sword belongs to a figure about that period. In 1534 he gives an example 'from the brass of William Asshery, Harefield, Middlesex.' It has a pommel of six flutings, a round cap with yet another button-like top. Now, none of those examples are the same as those of the Scottish swords. The latter are in every way far finer in beauty of line and contour.

The pommel of Argyll's sword in the monument at Kilmun is not peculiar to the Highlands.[1] It is that worn by English and French knights of the period. It may be well to turn to one well-known and valuable work representing Highland knights in plate armour, having swords of various patterns, and it is these swords that are peculiar and noteworthy, not the plate armour. As to colouring in this work, it is well to note that the artist had apparently a limited variety of colours. The heraldic colour 'gules,'= red, appears to have been applied alike to the cheeks and noses and to the tinctures of feathers used in the helmets; but, whatever may be the shortcomings of the coloration, the drawing of the swords is at all events noteworthy and curious.

[1] See Plate at beginning of Chapter IX.

Some years ago, the late proprietor of the Queen's Hotel, Glasgow, Mr. MacGregor of Glengyle, lineally descended from Rob Roy MacGregor, used to show persons who sojourned at his hotel the sword of the famous Rob Roy. It was a broadsword of very fine temper, and had a broad blade, and looked as if at one time it had been a two-handed sword. It was in the latter part of his life that Mr. MacGregor acquired Glengyle by purchase—ancestral lands which had been out of the hands of the MacGregors for many a long day. Rob was well known as a good swordsman; but, in speaking of this sword, it is well to turn to Stewart's *Sketches of the Character, Manners, and Present State of the Highlanders of Scotland*, Appendix, portion xxxvi. General Stewart has the following note concerning a son of Rob Roy's, James MacGregor :—

'A relation of mine, the late Wm. Stewart of Bohallie, afforded an instance of this [personal encounters, duels, and trials of swordsmanship]. He was one of the gentlemen soldiers of the Black Watch (but left them before the march to England), and one of the best swordsmen of his time. Latterly he was of mild disposition, but in his youth had been hot and impetuous; and as in those days the country was full of young men equally ready to take fire, persons of this description had ample opportunity of proving the temper of their swords, and their dexterity in the use of them. Bohallie often spoke of many contests and trials of skill, but they always avoided, he said, coming to extremities, and were in general satisfied when blood was drawn, and "I had the good fortune never to kill my man." His swords and targets gave evidence of the

service they had seen. On one occasion he was passing from Breadalbane to Loch Lomond through Glenfalloch, in company with James MacGregor, one of Rob Roy's sons. As they came to a certain spot, MacGregor said, " It was here I tried the mettle of one of your kinsmen "; some miles further on, he continued, ' Here I made another of your blood feel the superiority of my sword ; and here," said he, when in sight of Ben Lomond, in the country of the MacGregors, " I made a third of your royal clan yield to MacGregor." My old friend's blood was set in motion by the first remark ; the second, as he said, made it boil ; however, he restrained himself till the third, when he exclaimed : " You have said and done enough ; now stand and defend yourself, and see if the fourth defeat of a Stewart will give victory to a Gregarach." As they were both good swordsmen, it was some time before MacGregor received a cut on the sword-arm, when, dropping his target, he gave up the contest.'

'James Drummond MacGregor was implicated with his brother Robert in carrying off by force a rich widow, whom he afterwards married. For this crime they were tried and condemned. Robert was executed in 1753, but James escaped from prison and fled to France. " He very honourably rejected money offered to him to become an informer and spy for the French Government, and died in great poverty.'

CHAPTER VI

ROB ROY

Few battle-pictures are more astounding or strange than that brought to our notice by an eye-witness who watched the bearing of Rob Roy as he gazed on the battle of Sheriffmuir.

We have here placed on record the fact that Rob Roy headed a party of men, without any distinct idea on which side he had to fight; and whether from difficulty in getting men together, or from what other causes, he was late, as is well known, on the scene of action. This is the account given by the eye-witness :—

'I was one of two hundred men who accompanied Rob Roy, as we thought, to fight for King James; but fortunately for ourselves, as I am now convinced of our folly, we were a few hours late. When the valley of the Allan opened to our view, we saw a moving mass approaching us.

'The sun was shining bright; we could plainly see the red-coats of the rebels.[1] When their cavalry stuck in the fatal morass, as you are informed, we saw the dark mass formerly moving in front of them now began to extend, as it were, from two opposite points, and gradually formed a ring, which enclosed the scarlet cloud on all sides. Rob Roy looked

---

[1] King George's troops.

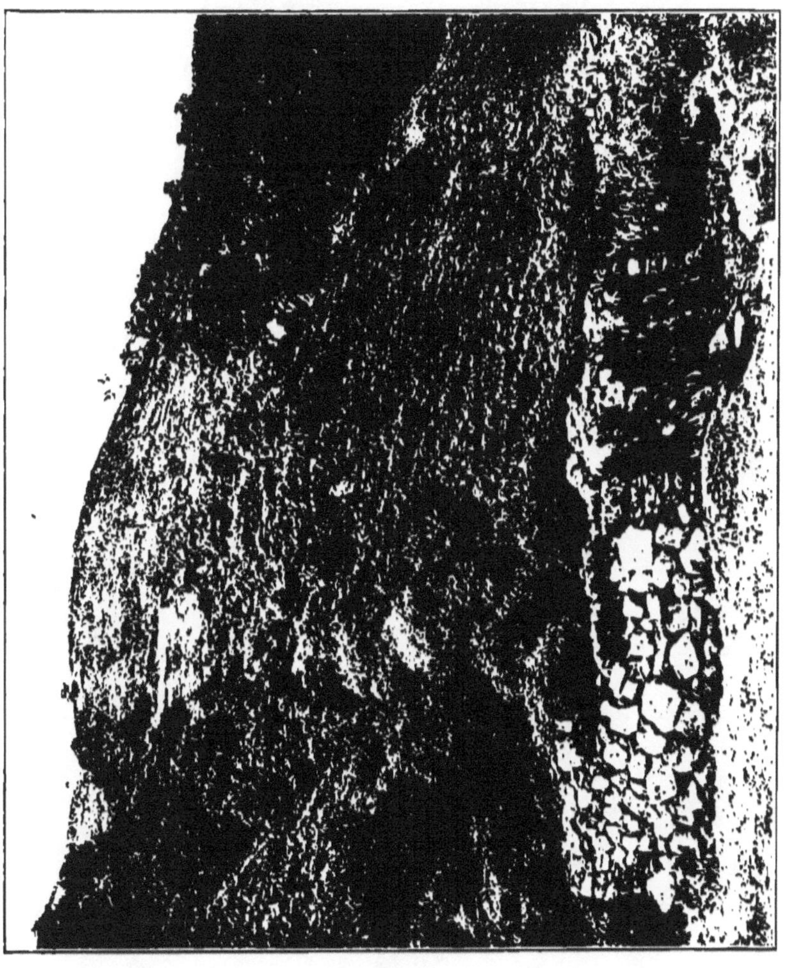

21. REMAINS OF ROB ROY MACGREGOR'S COTTAGE

attentively for some time. He appeared as if unconscious of
his being alive.

'He at last broke silence, looking around him in apparent
great anxiety, and said, "Gentlemen, will you fight for Mac
Cailein Mor?" at the hearing of which each man looked at his
fellow in sullen silence.

'He then asked, "Will you fight for Mar?" Each man drew
his sword, and exclaimed, "God bless King James."

'By this time we plainly saw that the struggle in the valley
below was fast coming to an end; for every second the red
mass enclosed in the dark ring was diminishing, till at last it
decayed into a mere speck, and finally disappeared altogether.
"Well," said Rob Roy, "that is so much. However, I think
it is not proper for us to fight, for neither King James nor for
King George; for my own part, I must say that both Mar and
Argyle were my friends at all times."'

It is well known that Rob Roy had obtained shelter
eight miles from Inveraray, but the date when he first
lived there is not known. But Argyll had some reason
to count on his services; this is evident from the first
question Rob Roy put. It is also probable he asked if
they would fight for the Duke's side, so as later on to be
able to say he thus fairly put the issues to his companions.

Whether Rob Roy was living under the Duke's protection at this time or not, Argyll could not have made
the blunder of asking him to 'come out'; but from
Rob's question it is more than likely that he was at that
time, so to say, a tenant of the Whig Duke. The
number of men raised in the very glen where Rob was
sheltered is recorded elsewhere:[1] these went out with the

------

[1] *Records of Argyll.*

Duke, and fought under him; the two hundred mentioned must therefore have been from other districts lying north and north-east of Inveraray.

To this day, though so much has been written about Rob Roy, few realise the fact that MacGregor was a man of education and a gentleman. No man of that time who was not thoroughly educated could have drawn up a paper such as Rob Roy drew up and signed. This is proved by documents now extant. That he was driven to desperation by brutal outrage committed on his wife in his absence is well known—outrage for which he knew he would and could find little or no redress. His handwriting is distinguished by its excellence. The spot he chose for a dwelling-place, some eight miles up Glen Shira, when living under Argyll's protection, is one of singular beauty and security. The wayfarer comes on it quite suddenly, after rounding one or two small hummocks. A path leads up to the ruins of the house from a beautiful natural gorge, full of tumbled-about, moss-covered granite rock, very much like the ground Salvator used to delight to paint as the haunts of freebooters of his own land. Rob and his men were wont to drive captured cattle down two straths—one southwest of Ben Buie and the other trending northward. The cattle were made to pass the house, and were kept safe in a rough natural tongue of land between two rushing streams. This tongue of rough land contains grass and heather, rowan or mountain-ash trees, and

22. ROB ROY'S TOMB

hazel and birch. A dyke at the base kept all secure, and on the flanks on either side wattle-fences were erected at any spot where the cattle could break through. There are places on the eastern side where people and cattle can easily cross over; on the western side, however, this is not possible, as the bank is precipitous. The whole scene is most beautiful and romantic. The keepers, and others belonging to the Inveraray district, used, when the roof-trees were still standing, to point out that these were put up MacGregor fashion, not in the manner known in the district. There were certain peculiarities in the jointing or laying and pinning the roof-trees together. All this wood-work has long since disappeared, but for many years the house was in good order, and, the same as in MacGregor's day, a wattled partition divided the dwelling part from that which was a byre. The interstices of this wattled partition were filled in, as usual in the Highlands, with cow-dung and moss.

At the back of the house the land slopes rapidly down to the stream, which is fringed with all the trees that go to make a natural wood in the Highlands —alder, rowan, birch, hazel, and blackthorn. The stream has worn deep cavities in the rock, and to the spectator standing in the bed of the stream and looking north the scene is one of greatest beauty. The rough footbridge in use still probably marks the site of a yet older one, which MacGregor must have used. It was not far from this bridge that a skian-dubh, or stocking knife, was found among the rushes some years ago, with Rob's initials cut on the horn handle, and which is in the Duke of Argyll's collection of curiosities at Inveraray.

MacGregor had another hiding-place a little up the glen, on the south-eastern side of Ben Buie. It is in the bed of the stream, and few people would suspect the place capable of housing anything larger than a badger or a fox. It is, however, large enough to shelter several persons at a pinch, or in times of great danger.

[illegible] most typical [illegible]

[illegible] _Arms of True Highlanders_ [illegible] Mr. [illegible]

[illegible] Highland arms [illegible] Plates

xliv. and xlv.

That represented in Plate xliv. belonged to Duncan

Forbes of Culloden, and was used at the Battle of

[illegible]den. It has a large central boss with circles

[illegible] on it, with small nails all round the outer rim

[illegible] Quite outside this, ornamented with small

[illegible] six circles, having small

[illegible] described in the [illegible]

[illegible]

[illegible] studs [illegible]

[illegible] the [illegible]

[illegible]

[illegible] dark [illegible]

23. HIGHLAND TARGET, FROM DUNOLLIE CASTLE.   20 INCHES IN DIAMETER

CHAPTER VII

TARGETS

Two of the most typical targets are those engraved in *The Book of True Highlanders*, Mr. MacIntyre North's valuable work on Highland arms, customs, etc., Plates XLIV. and XLV.

That represented on Plate XLIV. belonged to Duncan Forbes of Culloden, and was used at the Battle of Culloden. It has a large central boss with circles engraved on it, with small nails all round the outer rim—a star-like pattern outside this, ornamented with small nails—outside this again are six circles, having a smaller boss than the central one already described, in the centre of each of these circles. The pattern of these outer circles varies—two having a running scroll, two made with a star-like pattern, and the two others of U-shaped lines and curves. The spaces between these circles are filled with triangles, each three sides having a slight curve. Small studs or nails are placed in the centre of each triangle, and the triangles are marked out with smaller studs. The outer rim of this beautiful example has a double line with small studs.

The target represented on Plate XLV. has a large central boss with four projections like a sword point, an arrangement of triangles between each point, with a single line of studs at the base of each triangle, but the sides are marked by a double line of studs. Outside, or flanking these triangles, is a fine scroll bounded by a double line of studs. Outside this is another scroll design, again bounded by a double line of studs. The next space is filled by an interlaced scroll pattern. The outer rim shows a double circle of studs. The target shows a cross design formed of double lines of studs, thus dividing the shield into four parts. It is true that Indian targets show bosses somewhat similar, and Persian targets also show this arrangement, but the patterns and style of Celtic targets are quite peculiar.

There is an unfinished target in the Tower of London of a most beautiful and complicated design. The Perth Museum also has one of rare beauty.

The target of Stewart of Ardvorlich is also a splendid example.

I come now to two targets recently sent to the Edinburgh Museum by Colonel MacDougall of Dun-ollie. Dr. Anderson, the learned custodian, took casts of these beautiful examples, one of which has studs of silver, and is enriched by designs of the most beautiful pattern. They were discovered and brought to light by Mrs. MacNaughton, *née* Miss Campbell of Balleviolan, who found them neglected in an attic

24. TARGET FOUND AT DUNOLLIE CASTLE BY MRS. MACNAUGHTON,
IN AN ATTIC, COVERING SOME BARRELS

lumber-room at Dunollie House, two or three years ago.

They are among the most interesting specimens extant, the presence of silver studs being most unusual and noteworthy. It is needless to name all the other known examples. It suffices to say that one and all of the genuine Highland targets differ slightly in design.

The following account in the *Celtic Monthly Magazine*[1] is picturesque, and worthy of the notice of students of arms; but whether the theory that the cup-marks denoted the death of those fallen in battle remains to be proved :—

'The Gaelic shield was known as the *Sgiathballach*—Anglice, "the spotted wing," *ballach* being applied to these cups or bosses.

'What showed great skill in the armourers was—

'I. That each principal shield had a sound of its own, easily recognised, especially by the Bards.

'II. That some of the bosses also had sounds of their own.

'III. That necessarily all the shields must have been in harmony.[2] These qualities, both in shields and special bosses, enabled the king and his leading champions to signal to the whole host, or part of it, in presence of the enemy. For instance, Cathmore's shield had seven bosses, each of which had its own sound, and whereby he could signal to his own force.

'We now come to the uses that the shields were put to :—

'*First*—Before all others—was the guarding of the warrior from the swords, spears, and other weapons of his opponents.

---

[1] The author is indebted to the editor of the *Celtic Monthly* for permission to reproduce the account here given.

[2] *Celtic Monthly*, vol. i. p. 69.

'*Second*—Before starting on a campaign, for three nights the Bards sang the war-song in the hall of assembly, accompanied by the sounding of a shield.

'*Third*—Fingal was in the habit of devolving the command on one of his chief champions for the first day of the fight. A few of these were selected, who then took their position on the top of a knoll, and sounded their shields with all their might, and on the chiefs of the Bards fell the duty of fixing upon the one whose shield sounded the loudest. This they could do, as each shield had its own sound.

'*Fourth*—The great national shield was at such times hung up between spears, or two boughs of a tree, beside the commander's temporary abode. When the champion selected to lead on the first day failed in achieving more than a drawn battle, this shield was sounded to intimate to the host that the commander-in-chief himself would lead on the morrow. Fingal, as was his wont, would have intervened sooner if there was any risk of a defeat, but as there was not, he delayed so as to give the chosen leader every chance on that day.

'*Fifth*—It was sounded as a warning before the battle commenced.

'*Sixth*—During the advance, which was led by the Bards, chanting the march, occasionally the whole host broke in, striking their shields with furious battle-clang.

'*Seventh*—On the defeat of the enemy the host were recalled from the pursuit by the sound of the shield.

'*Eighth*—Cups from their shields were laid beside the warriors in their graves. Toscar and Ossian did so when raising a memorial stone to those killed in battle. It is not said that cups were also cut on the memorial stones, but it is certain that they were. These cup-marked stones and rocks are found over all parts of Britain inhabited by Celts, and it is our tradition that they were cut in honour of departed heroes. In Breadalbane, to my own knowledge, a cup-marked stone was almost invariably found near our burial circles. I had myself the satisfaction of opening a mound at Dalraoch, Fortingal, on which one of these stones had stood, and found therein the remains of a skeleton.[1] Sometimes it is a stone with one cup mark, as in this case, and sometimes it is a rock with a very large number of cups. The two finest specimens of this I have met with was at Craggantoll, in Breadalbane, and Almais Rock, in Yorkshire.

'Then the term *ballach* is both applied to shields and cup-marked stones. The invariable tradition of the Gaels is, as just said, that the cups were in honour of departed heroes. When on stones singly, they must represent one exceptionally distinguished hero, and when on rocks in great numbers, they must represent many heroes fallen in battle in some spot near by them. My explanation of the wherefore of the cup marks is intelligible, and, I think, satisfactory to any Gael who knows his own country thoroughly, with its history, annals, traditions, customs, names of places, and monuments. This intelligibility is very different from planet-worship and other imaginary theories of the haziest kind. The Gaels had no worship of the heavenly bodies. There was a race in our Gaeldom before we Gaels who *did* worship the sun and moon. This, too, seems to be nearly all we have got about them. Indeed, as far as I know, the skeleton which I found in the mound at Bruach, Glenlyon,[2] is the only nearly perfect one which has yet been found.

'The bossed shields and cup-marked stones are still more closely allied to each other by the type of design that characterises both of them. Thus we have a metal shield with but one circle of bosses at the circumference, and others with several concentric circles of alternate bosses and spaces from the centre to the circumference. One found at Harlech, in Wales, has a number of bosses irregularly placed within the centre circle, and seven concentric circles (but no bossed ones)

[1] *Proc.* Soc. Antiq. Scot. 1883-84, p. 376.
[2] *Ibid.* 1884-85, p. 39.

from thence to the circumference.[1]   We have also leathern
shields with the same manner of circles and spaces, the bosses
being represented by nails with brass knobs, and with spiral
and interlaced patterns on the spaces, as well as various other
devices—all of them, however, conformable to the circular and
circulo-spiral type of design.[2]   The finest specimens of cup-
markings that I have seen are in the neighbourhood of Ilkley,
Yorkshire; for instance, some single cups with one or more
circular lines cut around them, and clusters of cups, with spiral
lines entwining amongst them.

'There are some who hanker after the mystic, and find all
manner of superstition in these.   I see nothing in them but an
evidence of that sense of the beautiful and the heroic, which is
so important a part of the idiosyncrasy of the Celt, and especially of the Gaelic Celt.

'I have in my possession a very old family dagger, a Scotch-
made "Andrea Farrara," which
has a brass-plate at the end
of the handle with the ancient
arms of the Stewarts of Appin
engraved on it.   Opposite is
a copy of it from a drawing
made for me by my friend
Dr. Brigham, of London.

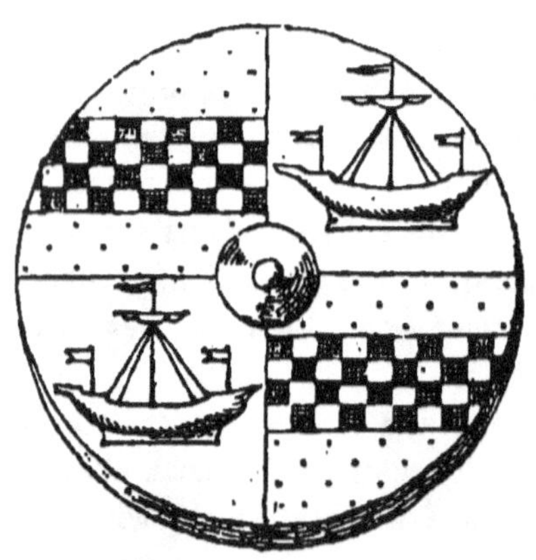

'The execution of the
original engraving shows how
old it is.   In each of two of
the compartments we have a
galley of Lorne.   In other
two we have the fesse cheque of the Appin Stewarts, representing
the order in which they fought, and which seems to me to be
a forestalling of our present mode of skirmishing.   Then we

---

[1] See *Stone Monuments*, by Waring (1878), plate 79.
[2] These, of course, are of a later period than the third and fourth centuries, but,
doubtless, the reproduction of the older designs.

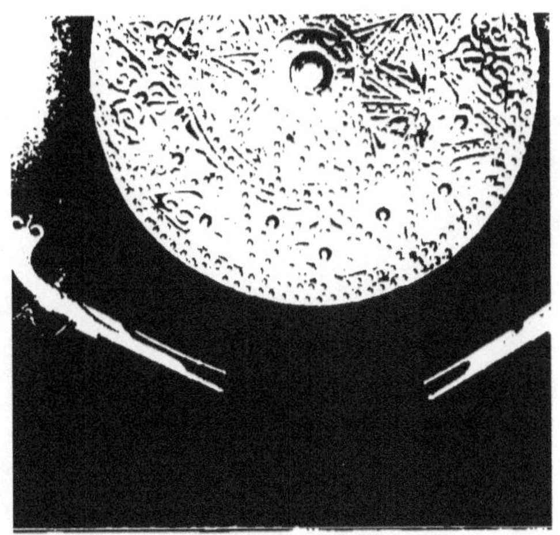

25. FROM THE QUEEN'S COLLECTION AT WINDSOR

have four compartments with cup marks. It is also interesting to state that the edges of this shield-representative are dented, like those of one which had seen service in the hands of a champion.[1] To have dents on the shield was honourable; to have it broken was looked upon as disgraceful. The Gael was from his infancy taught the use of the broadsword, and even so must it have been with regard to the shields, for unless he had the full knowledge and command of them he could not present the proper angle to receive the arrow in its flight, the spear in its cast, or the sword in its cut, and thus the shield would be broken. The most intensely beautiful use made of this cup-marking is by Ossian, in a notable passage, in which he tells us that this earth is to pass away, leaving nought behind it but a mist, on which is recorded by cups the deeds of the good and mighty. The word he uses as to this mist is *ballach*, which we have seen was applied to cup-marked rocks and stones, and also to shields. The cups on these represented, during the existence of time, glorious deeds done on this earth, whilst those on the mist represented the same deeds when earth and earthly time had passed away for ever. Such at least was Ossian's wondrously beautiful conception, flowing from the Gael's sublime belief in the spirit's immortality. For it may be asked, "But who would be there to see these cups?" Who but those Gaels whom he believed would, when their "spirits," or "I ams," parted from their souls and bodies, pass into a heavenly region, not of mere contemplative idleness, but of glorious activity.'

[1] Carried by Donald Stewart at Pinkie, 1547. See *Geneal. Stewarts of Appin*, by J. H. J. Stewart and Col. Duncan Stewart (1880), p. 168.

CHAPTER VIII

OF VARIOUS WEAPONS

THE plate containing specimens of dirks, swords, and pistols must be described in detail, as it contains an Andrea Ferrara which has an Indian hilt, and which has been 'mounted' in that country. It came with a lot of other fine swords to a merchant in London, who sold it to the writer in 1894. It may be best at once to describe the peculiarities of this splendid blade. It has no cross-and-ball mark on it at all. The name Andrea Ferrara is followed by a kind of cross of small size. The ornamentation along the back, three-quarters of the way towards the point, is that of a number of semicircles touching each other; above each semicircle are notches. This mark is of importance, and reappears on the beautiful example belonging to the writer which was shown at the Lyceum exhibition of swords and swordsmanship, given by Sir Henry Irving, in which Sir Frederick Pollock and Mr. Walter H. Pollock gave illustrations of attack and defence, together with Captain Hutton and other enthusiasts and lovers of 'the white arm.' This mark is known as the hog-back mark. The sword is remarkable

1. Dirk, having a blade notched, attributed by Seymour Lucas, Esq., R.A., to A.D. 1540.

2. Dirk, handle of ebony, blade made from an Andrea Ferrara sword.

3. Sword from the Sinclair Expedition, bought from a peasant of the district, 1894.

4. Dirk, late seventeenth century, handle of dark-brown wood.

5. Andrea Ferrara sword, hilted in India.   This sword came from India, 1894.

6. Scottish Broadsword, Highland type.

7. Long Highland pistol, purchased 1894 from a Swiss collection.

Various pistols.

CHAPTER VIII

OF VARIOUS WEAPONS

THE plate containing specimens of dirks, swords, and
pistols must be described in detail, as it contains an
Andrew [illegible] ... which [illegible]

[illegible]edly a kind of ancient small arm. The [illegible]
[illegible] pattern along the back, three-quarters of the way
toward the joint, is that of a number of semicircles
touching each other; above each semicircle are notches.
This mark is of importance, and reappears on the beautiful
example belonging to the writer which was shown at the
Lyceum exhibition of swords and swordsmanship, given
by Sir Henry Irving, in which Sir Frederick Pollock
and Mr. Walter H. Pollock gave illustrations of attack
and defence, together with Captain Hutton and other
enthusiasts and lovers of 'the white arm.' This mark is
known as the 'hog back mark.' The sword is remarkable

for its perfect balance when in the hand, and was inherited from Robert Campbell, Esq. of Sonachen. Mr. Seymour Lucas pronounces this to be a unique example. It has one broad shallow groove, and is noteworthy for the great breadth of blade.

The seventeenth-century short cutlass has a blade slightly curved, and is a weighty sword of somewhat coarse workmanship. The blade has a broad, shallow groove, with the armourer's mark, E.K., twice repeated, and an emblem in the middle between these marks, somewhat like a tiger's head looking full face at the spectator. The handle has a punctured quatrefoil, somewhat like the heart-shaped puncturing on a broadsword of Highland make. The weapon is figured in Meyrick, who christens it 'German' (vol. ii. Pl. CIII. fig. 17); whether it is or not remains ·to be proved. It has a curious rough pattern, a scroll, on the quillons. The story attached to the sword, which has never been in the trade, is that it belonged to Sinclair's force, which was overwhelmed by the brave peasantry of Norway. It came straight from the hands of a peasant to those of the writer as having belonged to, and being a relic of, the Scottish Expedition. It has received much damage, but shows the S-like quillons, and the punctures above spoken of; it has also been shortened or rounded off, and undoubtedly was originally of considerably greater length. Meyrick, in vol. iii. Plate CIII. No. 17, gives the type of weapon. He reckons the sword as belonging to the sixteenth century.

The date of the Sinclair Expedition was 1612. There are various statements as to the number of the Scots that accompanied Sinclair.

'In 1612, Gustavus caused foreign troops to be enlisted in the Netherlands, in England, and in Scotland, by Johan Munkhaven or Möunichhopen, a colonel in the Swedish service, and by James Spens, an Englishman. According to the historian Widikindi, the corps thus raised amounted to 2200 men, while Puffendorff estimates its strength at 2300. These troops, of whom 2000 had been recruited in Scotland, were transported in ships, forming two squadrons, of which one was commanded by Munkhaven, the other by the Scottish colonel, George Sinclair, or Saint Clair, as his name is also written. Munkhaven, with his 1400 men, steered into the Trondhjem fiord on the 19th July 1612, and thought he would be able to surprise the city of Trondhjem ; but the citizens opposed him and his ships so well from their blockhouses outside the town that he hastened away as quickly as possible, and landed at Stordalon, whence he marched, ravaging and burning, until he reached Sweden. A few weeks after Munkhaven, the other detachment of hired troops, led by Colonel Sinclair, arrived in two Scottish ships. But Sinclair and his men were not destined to escape so easily as Munkhaven. The fates ordained that they should all, with the exception of a few, find a grave among the mountains of Norway. The reason why both Munkhaven and Sinclair landed in Norway, instead of proceeding direct to Sweden, was that the approach to the small stretch of Swedish coast on the North Sea was closed to them after the Danes had occupied the fortresses of Elfsborg and Gullberg, at the mouth of the Gotha river. Moreover, the Danish fleet had the mastery on the seas.

'There are various statements as to the number of the Scots that accompanied Sinclair. If the total number of troops recruited for Sweden was, as already mentioned, 2200 or 2300, of which Munkhaven arrived with 1400, Sinclair's corps must have amounted to 800 or 900 men; and the latter number is also quoted in the church register of Vaage. Consequently, the number could not have been 1400, as sung by Storm, nor 600, as stated by Slange. It is, however, probable that Slange was right, as his statement agrees approximately with Kruse's report, which says that, according to the depositions of the Bönder who were present at the battle, and who buried and counted the dead and defeated, the Scots must certainly have numbered at least 550. Less probable appears to be the statement of the captured Scots, to the effect that they were 350 men strong at the utmost.'[1]

It was at the 'Kringelen' that the Bönder prepared to meet Sinclair and his Scots, and it was in the defile between the wooded hillside and the river that most of them were cut down or destroyed by a fall of stones and timber which crashed down from above them from a species of platform prepared by the peasants. Rocks and trees were hurled upon them by a cunningly prepared series of breastworks, the props of which were removed just as the Scots passed below. One hundred and thirty-four were taken prisoners, and all were shot in cold blood, with the exception of eighteen. The massacre in cold blood took place in a barn at a place named 'Qvam.'

The illustrations are not contemporaneous; that depicting the landing of the Scots shows a kilted Scot in the stern of one of the boats, also a piper. Bryan gives the dates of one of the artists, as follows, in his *Dictionary*

---

[1] See *Scottish Expedition to Norway in* 1612, by Thomas Michell.

of Painters: Tideman or Tiedeman, Philip, *b.* at Hamburg, 1657, *d.* at Amsterdam, 1705. The plate depicting the landing of the Scots is from a picture by Tiedeman and Gude. Bryan affords no clue as to the date of the work of Gude. The figures of the Scots show half armour, some with flat bonnets with single plumes and plaids, some with the morion of the period. The figure wearing a demi-suit of armour has boots and spurs; the piper has a kilt and sword. The work by Mr. Thomas Michell dealing with the Expedition is one of great interest, and was published by T. Nelson Paternoster Row, London, Edinburgh, and New York. It has a fine plate of the pistols alleged to have belonged to George Sinclair, and there can be no doubt that they are of the period. The writer has seen another fine pair with the same work. The butts have an oval shape, a little like Turkish examples; but the work on the barrel and ornamentation is Scottish. So much for the history of the disaster to Scottish arms. As to the sword, it came from the district; and the tradition concerning the same is not likely to be a concocted one.

The Highland broadsword shown in the same plate is a two-fluted Andrea Ferrara, and a good specimen of this type of sword.

The topmost dirk has a blade with three notches on the {back, and this type of blade Mr. Seymour Lucas considers to be of Henry VIII.'s date. The handle appears to the writer very early also, of a hard white wood, now browned with age. The dirk next to this one is of wood as black as ebony—it may be of ebony itself,—and has a plain brass flat top, as has the older dirk spoken of above. It is of interest as having a blade made from an Andrea Ferrara sword, the groove being in the centre, with the name Andrea Ferrara repeated all along the groove. This weapon is in its original state, and was in a collection sold at Edinburgh with a number of Highland things belonging to the late Mr. Davie of St. Fillans.

The dirk next in order was purchased in London, and is a fine example of a Highland weapon. It has silver pins or studs as ornaments in the handle, and has silver mounts on the shoulders.

The pistols shown are by J. Murdoch. Those with the rounded butts are of brass, with silver ornaments let into the same—very fine specimens of Murdoch's art. The other examples are nearly all of his make, with the ram's-horn butts. The placing of the so-called ram's-horn ornament at the butt end of the Highland pistol can be traced very far back.

In Monsieur G. R. Maurice Maindron's work, *Les Armes* (Paris, 1890), page 71 contains an engraving of a very early type of Celtic, or perhaps Gaulish, sword. The grip is of a swelling form, and very short, and instead of a pommel the hilt ends in two strongly rolled up spirals on either side of a central pin. This is exactly like the butt-end ornament of an early example of a Highland pistol in the author's collection.

Monsieur Maindron calls this spiral antennæ, and indeed the shape reminds one of an insect's antennæ rolled up. This pattern has been handed down to us, and became, later on, the so-called ram's-horn ornament, the spiral of many turns becoming one single strongly beat piece of steel.

The early Celtic, or perhaps Gaulish, weapon figured in Monsieur Maindron's work was found at Lincoln. Similar forms, he notes, have been observed in France, of which one example exists in the Museum at Rennes.

And now we come to the long pistol, which has a remarkable history. It was found by a London dealer in a Swiss collection. This collection, on the owner, Baron von Elsner, dying, was left to the nation on the express understanding that all that was Swiss should go to, and be retained by, the Swiss. That which was foreign, however, they apparently considered themselves at liberty to sell, and this pistol was sold to the dealer spoken of. It was sold in 1893, and belonged to the fifteenth-century castle of Schwandegg, between Winterthur and Constance. Mr. MacIntyre North gives a drawing in his *Book of True Highlanders* which is of the same make. It is enriched and ornamented with bands of silver, and has a pierced trigger button and a ramrod of peculiar make, also pierced. The lock and pan are engraved with a floral design, and on the lock-plate a name appears, the only letters of which remaining legible are 'H. W . . . .', a name of five letters apparently. The 'sight' nearest the stock is very high, being a deep slit or cut in an upturned, broadened part of the barrel, and the foresight is a small pin of common shot-gun pattern. The 'chase' of the barrel has five inlaid bands and half-bands of silver, the complete bands being at the muzzle end. The semi-bands at the stock end have a floral scroll engraved. The whole weapon is of steel, with exception of the abovenamed bands.

The small knife at the bottom of the Plate is a *sgian dubh*, or stocking-knife, which the late Campbell of Sonachen gave the writer, and which Campbell of Islay closely examined and declared to be of very ancient date.

Notice must here be made of a slight mistake in the text of a series recently produced on various regiments. In speaking of the 42nd Regiment, and referring to Plate II. illustrating the passage, the writer says, 'The sergeants retained their formidable Lochaber axes.' Now, this Plate shows the sergeant bare-headed, his bonnet in his left hand, and in the right is the *halberd*, not the Lochaber axe, which was of another shape.

It is quite correct, as will be seen in General Stewart of Garth's book, that at one time the sergeants had the

Lochaber axe. That this was the case will be seen by the alteration that took place under Lord John Murray. We read that, 'The sergeants were furnished with carbines, instead of the Lochaber axe or halberd, which they formerly carried.'[1] The two weapons are not alike, the halberd figured is the same as those at Inveraray, which were about eight feet high from the tip to the steel-shod toe-piece. The Lochaber axe, which doubtless was worn by the sergeants of the independent companies, was a very different weapon.

The halberd shown in the *Illustrated Histories of the Scottish Regiments* is the halberd used in the English army of that time.

The fire at Inveraray Castle destroyed the poles of these old weapons but not the heads, and these can be seen any day, duly labelled, at the Castle armoury.

At Inveraray also are two of the very much rarer Highland battle-axes—handy, murderous-looking weapons, with heads of very fine steel. One of them is axe-shaped, with a sharp, peaked bill on the other side. The other has a rounded axe-head, with a flattened, pike-like, projecting spike on the opposite side. The hafts or handles are covered with red velvet, and studded with brass nails. These escaped the fire from the accidental circumstance that the writer and the late Campbell of Islay put them up on a trophy in the outer or smaller hall, which was not touched by the fire.

[1] *Stewart of Garth's Book,* vol. i.

The arming of the Black Watch was not uniform, some wearing targes, others none. Mr. Harry Payne's admirable illustration is taken from a plate in Grose's *Military Antiquities*. This little correction may perhaps be made, as the true Lochaber axe resembles a salmon gaff on one side, and a long, formidable axe of two shapes on the other. Another shape has a bridle-cutting, reaping-hook sort of weapon on one side, an axe on the other. They are nine feet in height. There are specimens at the Tower of London—weapons taken from the Highlanders during the various actions and campaigns.

The only thing comparable to the Highland battle-axe is, perhaps, an old-fashioned seventeenth or eighteenth century alpenstock, a specimen of which the writer found and brought home from the Engadine. It has a beak-like piece of steel on one side, and a beautifully forged, curious hammer on the other. It would make a hole in armour as well as in ice, if wielded by a strong arm.

The Swiss instrument, so like the Highland weapon as to the spike or beak, is $38\frac{1}{2}$ inches in length.

The Highland battle-axe is figured by Logan, vol. i. page 313, and was called *tuagh-catha*.

Two soldiers of the Black Watch fought with Lochaber axes in 1743 before King George—that is, they gave an exhibition of the mode of attack and defence.

In Mr. James Drummond's beautiful work, *Ancient*

Scottish Weapons, the Highland battle-axe is shown on Plate xxxiii.—figures 2, 3, and 5 show the Tuagh shape.

This work contains also many examples of the Lochaber axe.

He thus describes the weapon, and his words had best be given :—

'Scottish Lochaber axe—the blade long and thin, carried on the shaft by two collars, of which the upper is forged with the blade and the lower riveted on ; the upper end of the blade waved, with the lower merely curved ; the edge curved, with the ends considerably beyond the length of the back of the blade. A stout, strongly recurved hook is inserted in the upper end of the shaft, and the butt is protected by a conical ferule, with knob at the end.'

The forms vary, but the above is an excellent description of the arm—than which none was more formidable.

In Mr. Drummond's book, Plate xxxiv. shows two short battle-axes, figures 1 and 2, which are identical with those at Inveraray Castle, and here Mr. Drummond calls these weapons Jedburgh or Jeddart axes. It is not likely that he would thus have named them had he seen those at Inveraray. According to the specimens of the Jeddart axe figured elsewhere, this weapon was of a different shape ; so, at least, the writer thinks. Mr. Drummond says the old City Guard of Edinburgh carried a weapon similar ; but the weapon the City Guard carried was a halberd, and those axes at Inveraray are not the

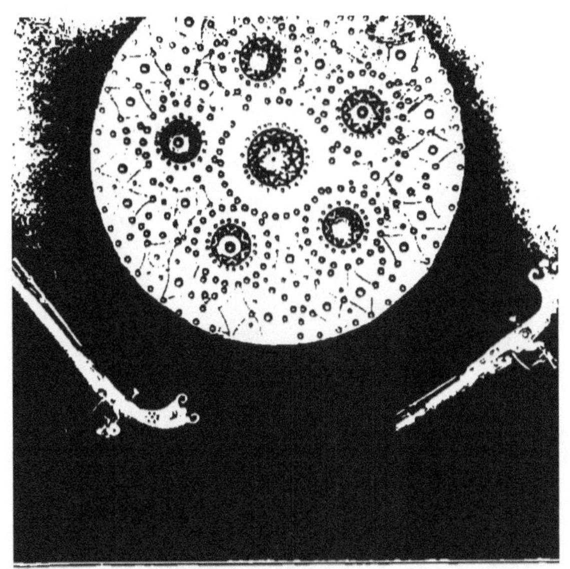

27. FROM THE QUEEN'S COLLECTION AT WINDSOR CASTLE

least the same in character. They are short, one-handed war-axes, with the most trenchant blades.

There is a very fine example of the dagger dividing into three in the Inveraray Armoury. When closed, it has the appearance of a broad dagger, but by pressing a spring made for the thumb the dagger divides. This weapon is elaborately engraved, and the hand is protected when on the grip by two steel prongs curving back toward the wrist when in hand. Each prong has a ball ornament at the end. It was only when Governor-General of Canada that Lord Lorne accidentally learned its history. He was asked by a Highlander resident in Canada whether the treble-bladed dagger was safe at Inveraray. He told Lord Lorne that it was found in Glenshira, among the tall brackens, and indicated the place on the hillside where it was found. The dagger would probably be classed as Italian in workmanship, and is probably sixteenth-century work. Up to the time of this statement being made we were not aware of the history of this fine weapon. The weapon is made of fine steel, there being no wood even on the handle, which is beautifully wired over. The engraving shows an Italian scroll design with pellet ornamentation on the pommel.

M. Auguste Demmin figures a dagger (p. 408, No. 28) in his useful book, and calls it 'Main gauche,' German, sixteenth century. It is represented in the following museums or collections :—Musée d'Artillerie,

Paris, and also in the Museums of Prague and Sigma-ringen.   (See the arms of the Free Judges.)

In M. Demmin's illustration the weapon is open, showing the blade divided into three parts or points; it also shows the strong spring between the main and the two side blades, which are much weaker than the central limb or blade.

It will be seen that M. Demmin calls this weapon a sixteenth-century weapon, to which conclusion the writer came from the make and style of ornament on the weapon found among the long brackens or fern at Inveraray.   It is of the time of Queen Mary, and it is not at all impossible that it was lost in some hunting expedition such as the Queen indulged and took part in when she visited her half-sister, the Countess of Argyll. M. Auguste Demmin says : ' It is probable that this weapon was used in administering an oath in the name of the Trinity.'   It is not very likely that the weapon was worn and reserved for such an object by the High-landers : it is much more likely that it was worn as being a weapon of fine make, and likely to make a speedy end to a quarrel.

28. SIR DUNCAN CAMPBELL, LORD OF LOCHOW, AND HIS WIFE MARJORY,
DAUGHTER OF THE DUKE OF ALBANY, AND FIRST COUSIN TO
JAMES I. OF SCOTLAND

28. SIR DUNCAN CAMPBELL, LORD OF LOCHOW, AND HIS WIFE MARJORY, DAUGHTER OF THE DUKE OF ALBANY AND FIRST COUSIN TO JAMES I. OF SCOTLAND

CHAPTER IX

OF ARMOUR

WE know from the monument at Kilmun on the Holy Loch, Argyllshire, that The Argyll, the first chief of the Campbells to assume the name Argyll, wore plate-armour of the same type as that found on the English monuments of that date, and the same as worn by the chivalry of most continental nations. This knight died 1453. These matters are named on account of the elaborate memorial erected to his memory. Tradition says that this monument was made in Rome. Some persons might think that the Highland knight was sculptured according to ideas and rules that obtained in Italy; but there is a detail on the breast-plate—namely, the gyrony of eight of the Campbells—that proves that Scottish eyes and orders superintended all, and saw that the effigy truly represented what the dead knight wore when fully armed for battle or for the lists. On his jousting helmet also is the crest of the Campbells—the boar's head of their ancestor Diarmaid. Special mention is here made of this monument because of the fashion of the armour. He wears the bascinet on his head, of slightly conical shape, with an orle,[1] pearl ornamented ; the mentonnière or chin-piece does not reach the lower lip ; the broad bawdrick or sword-belt, with its beautiful plaques, lies straight across the hips ; below this the jupon ends in a sort of trefoil pattern, formed of pellets. The chain-mail with the apex between the lip exactly in the centre ; the knee-pieces, (genouillières) ; the leg-pieces (jambs), cuisses, and the pointed toes (sollerets), with the superbly ornamented spur-straps, are almost identical with an example in Northleigh Church, Oxfordshire. The work is so much alike, that it seems evident, if the tale is true that this monument was made in Rome, that that of Northleigh Church, also of alabaster, may likewise have been made in the Eternal City. The head of Argyll rests cushioned on his tilting helmet, as in the case of the knight in Northleigh Church, Oxford-shire. There is another reason to think the workman-ship must be the same. The learned Skelton is full of just enthusiasm over the tomb of William Wilcotes, better known as Sir Ralph de Wilcote. He notes the superb detail of ornamentation. The pearls on the lady's head-dress, her splendid jewels, and the embroidery. No work was too elaborate for the artists of those brave days, and in the monument to Argyll and his lady all this detail re-appears. The Wilcote tomb is of a knight who died 1411, in the 12th year of Henry iv.'s reign.

---

[1] The orle was to take the weight of the tilting helmet from the head.

The ladies wear the same superb head-roll,[1] beaded with and wreathed with pearls and precious stones. The fashion of armour as worn by the Black Prince, who died 1376, to the date of the Wilcote tomb, about 1413, had not altered. The bascinet of William Wilcotes is of the same beautiful form, and the mode of attaching the ring-mail to the bascinet had alone been strengthened to prevent a sword-blow cutting the same. The date of the monument would be a little later than the date of death (1411). No monument so elaborate could have been wrought under two years. It is curious that the orle, richly ornamented, should have been worn by the ladies. It appears on the lady of Argyll's tomb, and on that of Wilcote. They were probably of silk, or cloth-of-silver or gold, pearl and precious-stone ornamented.

'This Argyll married, first, Marjory or Mariota Stewart, daughter of Robert, Duke of Albany, Governor of Scotland, by whom he had three sons. Celestine, the eldest, predeceased him; so did Archibald, the second, but he left a son; and Colin, who was the first of Glenorchy, and ancestor of the Breadalbane family. Sir Duncan married, secondly, Margaret, daughter of Sir John Stewart of Blackhall and Auchingown, natural son of Robert the Third, by whom he had three sons, namely Duncan, who, according to Crawford, was the ancestor of the house of Auchinbreck, of whom are the Campbells of Glencardel, Glensaddel, Kildurklane, Kilmorie, Wester Keams, Kilberry, and Dana; Niel, proprietor, according to Crawford, of the Campbells of Ellengreig and Ormadale; and Arthur or

---

[1] Head-roll or head-gear, a kind of wreath.

Archibald, ancestor of the Campbells of Ottar, now extinct. According to some authorities the Campbells of Auchenbreck and their cadets, also Ellengreig and Ormidale, descend from this, the youngest son, and not from his brothers.' [1]

This Argyll founded the Collegiate Church of Kilmun, and this has since his day been the burial-place of the Argylls.

The date of the assumption of the Galley for Lorn by The Argyll, the first Earl, was April 14, 1470.

Therefore no galley appears on the Kilmun monument, simply the Campbell gyrony. The way in which the galleys came on May 7, 1466 is as follows :—He obtained a confirmation of charter of Walter, Lord Lorn, to him of the lands of Kippen, Perthshire, and on the 10th of the same month a charter to himself and Isabella Stewart of Lorn, his wife, of the lands of Culdrane and Maid in Fifeshire and Innerdeny and others in Perthshire, on the resignation of Mariote Stewart, his wife's sister, and on the 8th February 1467 of the lands of Tanill in Perthshire. Having acquired the principal part of the property of the two sisters of his wife, the Earl entered into an agreement with their uncle Walter, Lord Lorn, on whom, as heir-male of the Stewarts of Lorn, the Lordship of Lorn and Barony of Innerneath stood limited, by which Lord Walter resigned the former to the Earl (who assumed the title of Lord Lorne, and took the Galley of Lorn into his own achievement),

---

[1] Keltie's *History of the Scottish Highlands*, vol. ii. p. 179.

29. BLAZON OF THE EARL OF ARGYLL, FROM ARGYLL HOUSE, STIRLING, NOW AT INVERARAY CASTLE, FROM A TRACING OF THE ORIGINAL, TRANSFERRED WHEN THE HOUSE BECAME A MILITARY HOSPITAL

… kinds of Caldrane

… members and others in P

ERLL OF ERGVLE

reserving to himself the title of Baron of Innerneath ; and on the 14th April 1470, the Earl obtained a charter of the whole lordship of Lorn to himself and the heirs-male of his body, with remainder to other members of his family, the Campbells of Glenorchy standing first, and the general remainder to the nearest heir-male of the Earl bearing the name and arms of Campbell.

The Argyll blazon was removed when the Argyll House was converted into a military hospital some years ago. The authorities sent this interesting relic to the present Duke of Argyll. It hung over one of the doors, and probably dates from the end of the sixteenth century.

The galleys are somewhat rudely executed, and there is no furled sail, it will be observed, from the cross-yard-arm.

In Sir David Lindsay's book the galley has a flaming beacon at the masthead, and the ropes are made out in somewhat similar fashion, but the poop or stern in the work of Sir David Lindsay of the Mount is more elaborate.

In later years the fiery tongues of flame from the beacon became a pennon at the masthead, with two smaller flags on staffs displayed at the bow and stern ; the sail, also, is furled from a beam, much the same as in use to our day by the boats using the 'lug' sail, and the four oars in action are added.

Whilst speaking of Lorn it will be as well to quote

the account given by. Sir Walter Scott of the way in which the Brooch of Lorn (so called) fell into the hands of the MacDougalls.   It had best be given verbatim :—

'Driven from one place in the Highlands to another, starved out of some districts, and forced from others by the opposition of the inhabitants, Bruce attempted to force his way into Lorn ; but he found enemies everywhere. The MacDougalls, a powerful family, then called Lords of Lorn, were friendly to the English, and, putting their men in arms, attacked Bruce and his wandering companions as soon as they attempted to enter their territory. The chief of these MacDougalls, called John of Lorn, hated Bruce on account of his having slain the Red Comyn in the church at Dumfries, to whom this MacDougall was nearly related. Bruce was again defeated by this chief, through force of numbers, at a place called Dalry; but he showed, amidst his misfortunes, the greatness of his strength and courage. He directed his men to retreat through a narrow pass, and placing himself last of the party, he fought with and slew such of the enemy as attempted to press hard on them. Three followers of MacDougall, a father and two sons, called M'Androsser, all very strong men, when they saw Bruce thus protecting the retreat of his followers, made a vow that they would either kill this redoubted champion, or make him prisoner. The whole three rushed on the king at once. Bruce was on horseback, in the strait pass we have described, betwixt a precipitous rock and a deep lake. He struck the first man who came up and seized his horse's rein such a blow with his sword as cut off his hand and freed the bridle. The man bled to death. The other brother had grasped Bruce in the meantime by the leg, and was attempting to throw him from horseback. The king, setting spurs to his horse, made the animal suddenly spring forward, so that the Highlander fell under the horse's feet ; and, as he was endeavouring to rise again, Bruce cleft his head in two with his sword. The father, seeing his

30. THE BROOCH OF LORNE

f these MacDougall
       of his havi
              ...
              ...
ers, at a ...
fortunes, the greatest
30 THE BROOCH OF LORNE
        of the party b...
             ... the ...
Dougall, his father and
strong men, when the
f his followers, made
  redoubted champio
ree rushed on the kin
e strait pass we have ...
a deep lake. He str...
t his horse's rein such
...d and freed the bride.

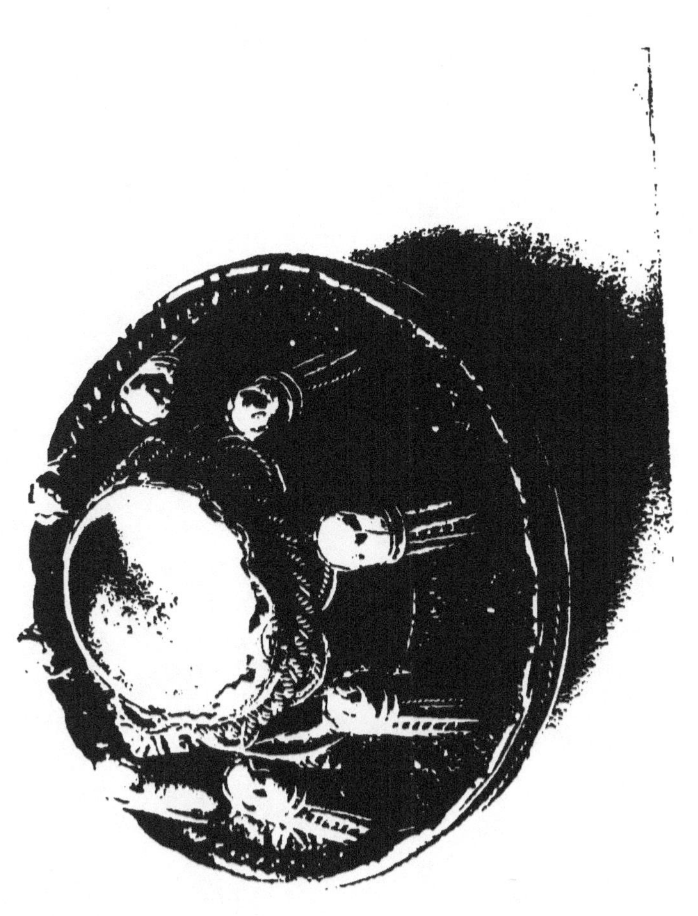

two sons thus slain, flew desperately at the king, and grasped him by the mantle so close to his body that he could not have room to wield his long sword. But with the heavy pommel of that weapon, or, as others say, with an iron hammer which hung at his saddle-bow, the king struck this third assailant so dreadful a blow that he dashed out his brains. Still, however, the Highlander kept his dying grasp on the king's mantle, so that, to be free of the dead body, Bruce was obliged to undo the brooch, or clasp, by which it was fastened, and leave that, and the mantle itself, behind him. The brooch, which thus fell into the possession of MacDougall of Lorn, is still preserved in that ancient family as a memorial that the celebrated Robert Bruce once narrowly escaped falling into the hands of their ancestor. Robert greatly resented this attack upon him, and when he was in happier circumstances did not fail to take his revenge on MacDougall, or, as he is usually called, John of Lorn.'

To the archæologist, and to all, this priceless relic must always remain an object of the deepest interest. The central stone is a crystal, and turret-like ornaments round the same have pearls at the apex. The photograph was sent to the writer by Colonel MacDougall to be reproduced for this work.

His father, the gallant Admiral, on hearing that the then Crown-Princess of Prussia, our Princess-Royal[1] (who was visiting the Duke and Duchess of Argyll at Inveraray), would like to see the Brooch, at once started off to Dunollie, and was back with the Brooch before dinner, a drive of over eighty miles. He was then well advanced in years.

---

[1] The Empress Frederick.

CHAPTER X

OF MONUMENTS AND THEIR EMBELLISHMENTS

ALTHOUGH shields bearing devices are not by any means always found on the tombstones in the West Highlands, there are many bearing the same—inasmuch as 'the earliest of these heraldic embellishments of shields may be said to have been in the reign of Richard I.'[1] We can approximately reckon the dates of the tombs of the knights having such 'heraldic embellishments.' At Innishael, Lochow, there is a tomb bearing a shield (see No. 2, p. 7, Boutell, taken from the Percy monument at Beverley, A.D. 1350) the shape of which should go far towards determining the date of the monument. Of course the shape that was in fashion in 1350 continued to be used. It is the same, or much the same, as that of the Black Prince at Canterbury, now hanging above his tomb; broader, perhaps, in make, but the same as to style.

There are also valuable lessons to be learned from the beading round the tombs—framing them, so to say. The nail-head, the star (four-pointed), the 'dog-

---

[1] See Boutell and Aveling, *Heraldry.* London: W. W. Gibbings, 18 Bury Street, 1892.

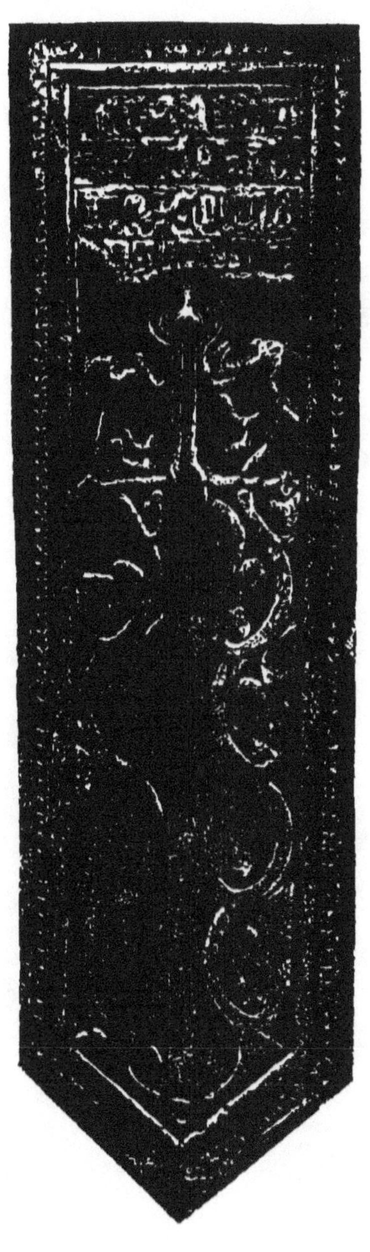

31. MAC CALIEN MHOR'S TOMB AT KILCHRENAN, LOCHAWE

32, TOMB AT ORANSAY PRIORY

33. TOMB AT ORANSAY PRIORY

tooth' pattern, like a four-leaved flower, and others of Norman origin, are most frequently met with. A beautiful example of the nail-head ornament, the nails being contiguous, will be found in the tomb, Plate 10 in Graham's *Iona*. This tomb, of MacDonald of Islay and Kintyre, is of importance as fixing the period of the most beautiful designs found in the Western Highlands. This knight was with Bruce at Bannockburn—fought 1314. The galley is very peculiar, and the sail is furled in a horizontal line half-way up the mast, the high-pointed bow and stern of the galley being a little higher than the furled sail. Below the galley are four rampant animals—lions and winged griffins, whose tails develop into beautiful interlaced designs, nearly all the leaves being trefoil pattern on a large scale. The banner is 'displayed,' the edge furthest from the pole terminates in the raven-wing, tongued or serrated. In the famous Bayeux Tapestry, the work of Queen Matilda (1066), this type of banner appears—namely, a banner having an edge divided into three prongs, or having a raven-wing appearance.

The MacDonald banner of Bruce's day has four spear- or sword-point-like terminations. The banner was apparently stuck upright between the mast and the prow. The effigy of the Earl of Argyll, buried at Kilmun, shows him clad in complete plate-armour, having a tight-fitting jupon embroidered with the Campbell gyrony, and he wears the knightly bawdrick, with square or oblong plaques. These bawdricks, or sword-belts, of the Middle Ages, are direct descendants of Roman models. The metal 'plaques,' fixed to the leather foundation or strap, are shown as worn by a Roman soldier of the iv. Cohort = Dalmatian, in a bas-relief in the Museum of Artillery, Paris. The plaques here are more oblong than square, having an ornamental design on each plaque. The bawdricks worn by the kings, nobles, and knights in the reign of Edward iii., sumptuous works of art, are but lineal descendants of the Roman sword and dagger belts. In this example the short sword hangs on the right hip and the dagger on the left side. (See Jacquemin's *Costume* ; Military— Infantry—Western Empire.)

Those who have seen the numerous ruins of churches on the Adriatic shores note that the interwoven runic knots and foliated patterns are common, and in some cases identical with knotted or interwoven patterns found on sepulchral slabs on the West coast of Scotland, and on monuments throughout Great Britain. The place of birth of such art is hard enough to trace with exactitude, but we need not go further east than the Mediterranean for the place of its origin ; for, if the unchanging Far East was the birthplace of such patterns, we should find the same in our day on buildings or in fabrics. Such is not the case apparently either in Persia, India, Arabia, the Holy Land, or Egypt.

34. TOMBSTONE FROM THE PRIORY CHURCH, ORANSAY

35. TOMBSTONE FROM THE PRIORY CHURCH, ORANSAY

The only example of interlacing pattern resembling work on the Iona stones in the East, and which came under the writer's notice lately, is of sufficient importance to record.

In looking over a series of photographs of buildings in and around Jerusalem, a very remarkable example is shown of a knotted pattern running along the entire length of a stone at the entrance of one of the buildings.[1] It resembles the scroll patterns bordering many of the manuscripts in the Bodleian Library at Oxford, and in thousands of other collections. It is the same as many of the patterns said to date from Druidic days, and affords the Celtic scholar ample food for study and reflection.

Did the sculptor borrow his design from the West, or have we borrowed from the East? Why should the knotted scroll pattern appear at Jerusalem, and not in neighbouring lands?

The carpets of the East, with all their thousand patterns, contain no trace of such design as we find on Christian tombs of the fourteenth or fifteenth centuries. That the monks brought these designs from the East may be the case as regards lands lying east of Great Britain ; but they do not belong to the Far East, with its unchanging customs and art traditions.

Speaking of the elaborate interlaced ornamentation on the monuments to be found in eastern Scotland, and

---

[1] Fountain near gate of chain, chief entrance to the Haram, Jerusalem.

on those of the west coast, Dr. Anderson concludes thus (*Scotland in Early Christian Times*, p. 132) :—

'And now I sum up the whole bearings of the evidence, whether derived from the general features or from the special art characteristics of these monuments, in one generalisation.

'They are monuments of Christian character and Christian time.

'There is no evidence to show that there was among our forefathers any pre-existing or Pagan custom of erecting such sculptured monuments in honour of the dead.

'The art which is found with Pagan interments is chiefly exhibited in connection with the plastic material of which they formed the urns deposited with their dead.

'On these frail vessels of clay the decoration consists invariably of simple linear patterns, formed of groups of parallel or obliquely disposed lines. Interlacements, circles, divergent spirals, and fretwork are totally unknown, and there is no approach to a scroll or running pattern of any kind but a simple zigzag.

'When their ornament appears on stone, which is of rare occurrence, it is seldom indeed that it appears in such a position as to warrant the inference that it was either intended to be seen, or to mark the place of interment in the manner of a monument.

'This may have been the purpose of the cairn raised over the grave which contained the decorated urn, or of the stone circle set up around a burying-place. But the art of the pre-Christian sculptor is more usually concealed than displayed. We may find the cover of the cist, a rude unshapely block, sculptured on its under side with cups and circles, or with triangles and rudely formed spirals. But we have never found in Scotland any monument erected over a Pagan grave which exhibits the least approach to a truly artistic decoration. The

36. A KNIGHT'S TOMBSTONE AT ORANSAY

37. TOMB AT ORANSAY

custom of erecting such monuments is Christian and Christian only, so far as Scotland is concerned, and the art they exhibit and the letters they bear were brought into this country with the copies of the Gospels from which Christianity was taught to the people.'

And now we come to Dr. Anderson's very just appreciation of all this lovely Celtic art as handed down to posterity :—

'I have shown that the art of the monuments was a peculiar development of the art of these manuscripts, confined to an unusually restricted area. But within that area it was largely developed. We have no means of judging of the extent of its practice, except by reckoning up the sparsely distributed examples that are left. It is clear that the number thus computed from casual and accidental discoveries must fall far short of the whole number that originally existed. Yet upwards of three hundred separate monuments can still be enumerated. Three hundred examples of an art like this represents a collection of art materials such as has not fallen to the lot of any other nation of northern Europe. They are materials of such intrinsic value and suggestiveness that our designers, sculptors, and jewellers are willing to borrow inspiration from them.'

Dr. Joseph Anderson says truly that no other northern nation has greater art treasures than has our Scotland. Whether we take the wondrous patterns for models to be used for jewellery or for wood-panel or stone-work, we cannot do better than study the beauty of this Celtic art, ever varied, never monotonous, well repaying the student and the artist's closest study.

It is not too much to say that there is a mine of

art-wealth in most of the Highland churchyards where sculptured stones are to be found.

Perhaps no paragraph in Dr. Joseph Anderson's work, *Scotland in Early Christian Times*, is more important than that on page 120. Speaking of a figure of an animal, something like a horse, with a long snout, its feet ending in curved lines, its tail terminating in the same way, and having a crest sweeping over its back from the forehead with the same scroll termination, and the centre of the figure being filled in with a Celtic scroll of fine design, he says :—

'Even the symbols, which may be regarded as of minor importance, are filled with ornament. But the forms as well as the decoration of these conventional symbols are also peculiarly Celtic. No such forms as those of the composite symbols of the double disc, the crescent, the horse-like figure, and the serpent, combined with the zigzag or V-shaped rod with floriated ends, are found in the Christian art of any other people. No form of cross created by any other art is the same as the Celtic form. And it is a very remarkable fact in the art aspect of the question, as apart from the question of symbolism, that no cross of the Celtic form, which is also decorated with pure Celtic ornament, bears any representation of the Crucifixion.'[1]

This is an error. In Graham's *Carved Stones of Islay* there are several examples of crosses with the crucified Christ.

The very archaic figure of a man's head surmounting a rude cross, at Killoran, Colonsay, is four feet five inches in

---

[1] *The Carved Stones of Islay*, by Robert C. Graham. See Plate XIII. fig. 39, Plate XV. fig. 52, Plate XVI. fig. 50, Plate XVII. fig. 53.

38. STONE CROSS AT ORANSAY

39. TOMB AT ORANSAY, SHOWING THE GALLEY, SWORD, KNOTTED
SCROLL PATTERNS, AND TREFOIL ORNAMENT

40. TOMBSTONE WITH ARCHAIC CROSS, TERMINATING
WITH A MAN'S HEAD

length, and must be reckoned as a very early type of monument. This figure is given in Dr. Anderson's work.

Speaking of the symbols carved in various caves known to have been the retreat of various saints—St. Serf's cave, for example, which was long a resort for pilgrims—he says :—

'The reason why these caves bear sacred symbols upon their walls must therefore be that they possessed a sacred character from traditional association with early saints. We see that one has been fitted up as a chapel, and that others have been apparently places of frequent resort. That places thus frequented for religious exercises should bear religious symbols is only to be expected. That those here carved, whose meaning is known, are religious in character and significance, is certain. That those whose meaning is unknown are different in character cannot be presumed in face of the fact of their appearing in the same association, alike on the monuments and in the caves, which practically and symbolically were churches. But these symbols also occur on metal-work, as well as in other situations, which neither connect them necessarily with religious nor with sepulchral usages. They occur graven on the terminal links of massive silver chains of double links which have been found in different parts of Scotland, ranging from Inverness-shire to Lanarkshire. They are found on silver pins of peculiar shape, which also bear the symbol of the Cross, although they are articles of dress or personal decoration. They have been found on plaques of silver and bronze, which are connected by the character of their art with the art of the monuments and manuscripts, although we cannot say of their purpose whether it was sacred or secular. But seeing that these symbols were in their nature such as could be appropriately used on articles of personal adornment, on costly articles like these massive chains,

while they were also appropriately carved on the rough walls of
seaside caves, and elaborately sculptured on monuments of
high artistic design, it is clear that they were of the widest
possible application, and must, therefore, have had a significance
unrestricted by local, personal, or official considerations.'

In *Ecclesiological Notes on some of the Islands of
Scotland* Mr. T. S. Muir gives the following concerning
Colonsay-Oransay.   Our illustration is of the remains
of the priory church ; but a passing notice concerning
the Isle of Colonsay is needful.

'These two islands, narrowly divided from each other by a
sound, passable on foot at ebb tide, are easily visited from Port
Askaig in Islay. At Killoran and Kilchattan, in Colonsay, were
religious houses. Of that in the former, said to have been an
abbey founded by St. Columba, nothing is left. At Kilchattan
there are slight remains of a chapel, a burying-ground, and two
standing stones called Carraghean.

'In Oransay are the remains of the priory church of the
Colonsay Cœnobium, a greatly wasted building with First- and
Second-Pointed features, internally about seventy-eight feet in
length. The east end is entire, and contains a plain unequal
triplet under a pointed arch with a trigonal dripstone. Under
it, inside, the altar, incised at the corners with a small cross, is
preserved. The domestic buildings were on the north and
north-east ; scarcely anything of them remains, though no
further back than Pennant's time they were almost entire.

'Around and within the church are some interesting monumental slabs, and a very fine cross, of the ordinary Argyllshire
patterns. The slabs are in most part sculptured with ecclesi-
astical and military figures in high relief. The cross—twelve
feet in height—has on its west face the Crucifixion, occupying
the disc and a part of the shaft, foliage enclosed in a series of

41. EXAMPLE OF CELTIC ARCHITECTURE AT ORANSAY PRIORY

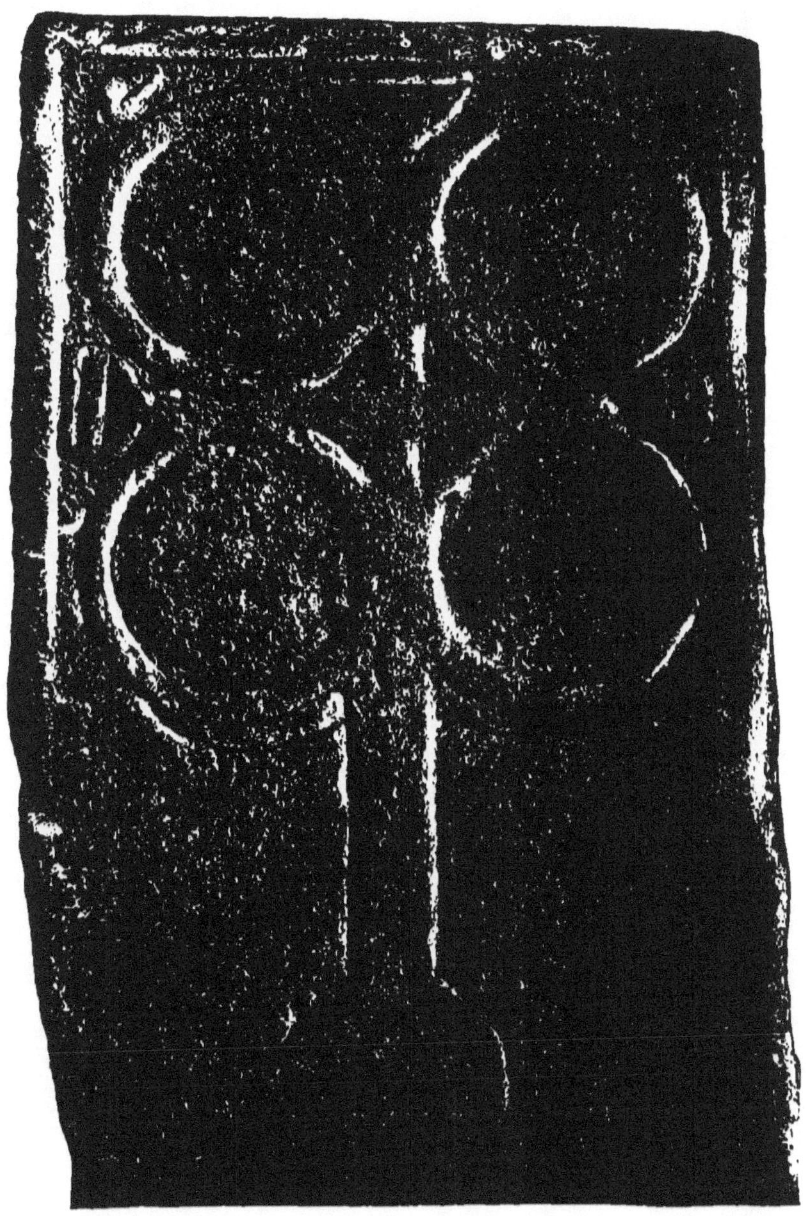

42. IN THE PRIORY CHURCH, ORANSAY

linked circles, and a faded inscription, commencing: *Hic : est : crux : Colini* : — the prior, no doubt, who is stated to have died in 1510; the east face of the disc is overspread with ornamental radii, the stem with leafage in circles, and two non-descript animals. Standing north-east of the church is part of the shaft of another cross, three feet in height, one of its faces worn smooth, the other covered with broad-leaved foliage. The disc is lying near it, one of its faces filled with the figure of an ecclesiastic, boldly relieved within a trefoil-headed niche.'

The reader will see from the illustration the style of architecture here treated of. The photograph was selected as giving the relative proportions of the human figure to the building.

The owner or laird of these beautiful islands is Major-General Sir John Carstairs M'Neill, V.C., K.C.B., K.C.M.G., one of the very few Gaelic-speaking landed proprietors.

A paper by the Rev. G. F. Browne, now Canon Browne, published in the Disney Series of Lectures, is too important to be left out. In treating of sculptured stones found in Derbyshire, he gives plates from rubbings of the crosses found at Bakewell. Now, these contain horses and horsemen of a type so very similar as to workmanship and style with those found at Iona and throughout the Western Highlands, that all these plates are worthy of the closest study. The Canon here speaks of dates :—

'It may be well to mention the English sculptured stones to which a date may be assigned by means of an inscription.—

The great column at Bewcastle (Cumberland) bears among other inscriptions a sentence commencing, " In the first year of Ecgfritte," and reciting that it was in memory of Alchfritte. King Ecgfritte succeeded Alchfritte in 664. At Hackness (York) are very interesting fragments with inscriptions in runes and in Latin characters of the date of the Lindisfarne Gospels. The most loving mother Ordilburga is named in one of the Latin inscriptions, and Bede tells us that King Aldfritte summoned his sister Ethelburga from the Abbey at Hackness to his deathbed at Driffield.   He died A.D. 705.'

Further on we come on a passage concerning the country whence this art was probably taken.   The Canon has the following :—

' In the Chapter library at Durham are two shafts from Hexham, which exactly suit the description of the two stone crosses set up to Bishop Acca, Mirabili Celatura, in A.D. 740.   While the Lindisfarne Gospels were being written, a cross was carved and set up in the island, so beautiful that it was carried away by the monks when they left.   William of Malmesbury gives a description of two very lofty obelisks at Glastonbury, with human figures in various robes, arranged in panels, and bearing their names, evidently Saxon ; and he describes the tomb of the Northumbrian abbot Tica, who fled before the Danes, as remarkable " *arte celature*," *as though he had brought the fashion from the North.*'

No one has taken a more complete survey of the sculptured stones to be found in this country, in Lombardy, and elsewhere, than Canon Browne, and the plates he gives of patterns found at Como are certainly akin to Celtic patterns.   The horses carved on many of the West of Scotland crosses and tombs look much like the

43. TOMBSTONE IN PRIORY CHURCH, ORANSAY

44. IN THE PRIORY CHURCH, COLONSAY
Details of Plate enlarged

45. LETTERING ON PLATE 43 DRAWN OUT BY MR. WILLIAM GALLOWAY

46. FIGURE OF AN ECCLESIASTIC ON A TOMBSTONE, ORANSAY

horses we see in tapestry of the period of the Conquest. Whatever be the date of the Bakewell shaft, it is impossible to pass these over. The style of sculpture is simply identical; the delineation of the horse is one and the same, but the head-dress and armour of the riders are different.

Captain T. P. White, in his *Archæological Sketches in Scotland*, has notes of immense value on all points. Of inscriptions, he notes that in the monuments of the West no Norman-French is met with. You rarely get more that *Hic Jacet*, followed by the man's name or individual's name: 'It is rare to meet, save in Iona, with any sentence running thus even—"*Hic Jacet* Robertus de Highmor cujus anime proficietur Deus," —to whose soul may God be precious. Again, as to symbols, the emblem of the key is more rare in the tombs of the West Coast, though this emblem is common on English tombstones, together with the shears.'

The Trinity is represented on crosses and tombs in various ways: the mystic number of three appears in three eggs in a nest on the central boss of the head-piece of the cross. This number is shown in the leaves of plants bearing a three-leaved pattern or trefoil, or sometimes the iris or common 'flag' in flower, with its *fleur-de-lis* head on the recumbent tombs. Of all parts of Argyll, Knapdale appears to be the very richest in monuments in good preservation. The detail of swords is very wonderfully preserved on many monuments, allowing us to study the ornaments down to the scabbard 'chape' or point.

The plates of tombstones, and in one instance of church or chapel architecture, are given to illustrate the types of ornamentation formed on Celtic memorials, also to show the various types of sword used by the Highlanders of old.

Many of these are from the Isle of Oransay, on the west coast of Argyllshire.

47. DUNFALLANDY CROSS, NEAR PITLOCHRY

Photographed by W. L. NASH, F.S.A., from Drawing by E. TOWRY WHYTE, F.S.A.

47. DURRAH KUV GROUP, NEAR JELALGENAT

Photographed by W. L. Merni, I.S.M. (Indr Drawing by R. Toula Whyte, F.S.A.

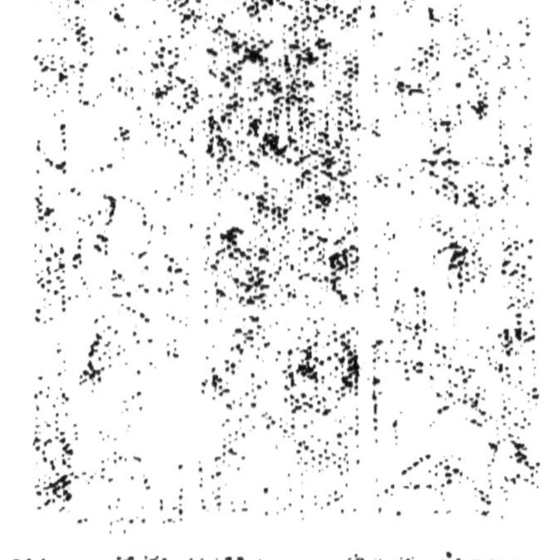

48. *Supporters of the arms of Skene of that ilk, 1672.*
From " Alexander Nisbet's Heraldic Plates."

CHAPTER XI

CONCERNING HIGHLAND DRESS

EXAMPLES of the wearing of the kilt in the seventeenth century are given in this work. The foolish reports made in 1785 can readily be discarded. The tale concerning the Englishman having invented the 'little kilt' is no older than 1785, and the passage may as well here be quoted (Pennant, vol. i. p. 210) :—

'The breachan consists of twelve or thirteen yards of narrow stuff wrappen round the middle. The truis was worn by the gentry, and was breeches and stockings in one piece. The feilebeg is a modern substitute for the lower part of the plaid.

'Thomas Rawlinson, an iron smelter and an Englishman, was the person who, about or prior to A.D. 1728, introduced the pheliebeg, or short kilt, worn in the Highlands. This fact, very little known, is established in a letter from Ewan Baillie of Oberiachan, inserted in the *Edinburgh Magazine* for 1785.

'The kilted plaid was the original dress. It is precisely that of a savage, who, finding a web of cloth, had not the skill to form it into a garment, but wrapt one end round the middle and threw the rest about his shoulders ; and it is little to the honour of Highland ingenuity that, although the chief wore long pantaloons called trews, the common Gael never fell upon any substitute for the belted plaid till an English officer, for the benefit of the labourers who worked under his directions on the military roads, invented the filibeg,' etc., etc.

Now the writer of all this rubbish was not aware, of course, that the Earl of Moray of Charles I.'s day, *inter alia*, wore full Highland dress, long before the period treated of here. And he asserts that the gentry did not use it!

The evidence of Sir William Sacheverell, Governor of the Isle of Man, is most interesting, and we can perhaps gather more from his than from any other account of what the armed Highlander looked like. He wrote (1688) concerning the Highlanders in Mull.

Again, the account given (1715) in the *Memoirs* of Marshal Keith, clearly indicates the dress of the men fighting in the Highlands :—

'At the battle with the Duke of Argyll (John, second Duke of Argyll and Warwick) a number of men lost their clothes. To explain this, one must know the habits of the Highlanders, and their manner of fighting. Their clothes are composed of two short vests, the one above reaching only to their waist, the other about six inches longer, short stockings, which reach not quite to their knee, and no breeches : but above all they have another piece of the same stuff, about six yards long, which they tie about them in such a manner that it covers their thighs and all their body when they please, but commonly it is fixed on their right shoulder, and leaves their right arm free. This kind of mantle they throw away when they are ready to engage, to be lighter and less encumbered.'

This means they wore the kilt, and that the heavier plaid was cast away—that is all. The word 'mantle' means plaid. The Highlanders did not cut this from the rest of the garb on the spur of the moment; it was a separate part of the dress. So much for the ridiculous nonsense published in the *Edinburgh Magazine*, for Baillie's wonderful discovery, and for Pennant's tale.

Keith's *Memoirs* antedate this tale. The plate of the arms of Skene shows the little kilt; and though the anatomy of the figures cannot be called good, yet the dirk and claymore in the hand and at the thigh of one of the figures are quite correct, and furnish one with the fact that the dress is fairly accurate also.[1] Another plate is given of two figures (kilted) of the seventeenth century wearing the small kilt. Much comment is needless with these ocular demonstrations at hand. Many evidences have turned up since Pennant's day to confute much that has been falsely asserted from Pennant's days to our own.

In the Introduction to the Nisbet Plates,[2] the work from which the illustration is taken, it is pointed out that in the Nisbet MS. the description of the supporters runs as follows :—

' Supported on the dexter by a Highland gentleman in his proper garb, holding a skein (dirk) with his right hand in a guarding posture, and on the sinister by another Highlandman in a servil habit, with his target on his left arm and his douloch by his side.'[3]

---

[1] Extract from *Old and Rare Scottish Tartans*, by Donald William Stewart. Edinburgh, George P. Johnston, 1893.

[2] *Alexander Nisbet's Heraldic Plates, originally intended for his System of Heraldry*. Waterston and Sons, Edinburgh, 1892.

[3] Nisbet MS., Advocates' Library, pp. 33-35.

It is impossible to conceive of evidence of a more conclusive and satisfactory character than that here adduced of the existence of both modes of dress at this period, and of the rank of the respective wearers. The original illustration is the work of Robert Wood, an Edinburgh engraver, and in Mr. Ross's opinion was executed, and Alexander Nisbet's description above quoted written, 1695-1704.

At Kilkerran or Kilkiaran, where Aidan, the most renowned of the Dalrendinian kings, is said to have been buried A.D. 605, there is a curious monument on which are two figures in a panel, one having a very decided kilt. It is said to represent a marriage.

The other kilted example is on a broken slab at Saddell Church. It represents a warrior, spear in hand, having a sword and kilt. No attempt has been made to touch up these rubbings.

'Saddell Monastery was organised by Somerled, carried on and completed by Reginald, his son and successor. It is one of the most beautiful places in the Highlands, situated in a wood-strath with a fine stream passing its former walls, over-shadowed on one side by fairly high hills all richly wooded.

'Tradition says Reginald, after his father's death, sent to Rome for a quantity of consecrated dust, and made the building commensurate with the extent to which it could be scattered. The building was in the form of a cross. Its length from east to west was about 136 feet by 24, and of the transept from north to south 78 feet by 24. The south end of the transept was extended from a gable to a distance of 58 feet, and from this projected another building running parallel to the

49. KILTED FIGURES ON MONUMENT AT KILKIARAN, CAMPBELTOWN, LOCH

It is impossible to conceive of evidence of a more
conclusive and satisfactory character than that here
adduced of the existence of both modes of dress at this
period, and of the rank of the respective wearers. The
original illustration is the work of Robert Wood, an
Edinburgh engraver, and in Mr. Ross's opinion was
executed, and Alexander Nisbet's description above
quoted written, 1695–1704.

At Kilkerran or Kilkerran, where Aidan, the most
renowned of the Dalriadan kings, is said to have
been buried, are, there is a curious monument on
which are two figures . . . . . . having a

. . . . a sword or spear in hand.
. . . . . . kilt . . . no attempt having been made to
set up these feelings.

. . . . Monastery was organised by Somerled, carried on
and completed by Reginald his son and successor. It is one
of the most beautiful places in the Highlands, situated in a
wooded strath with a fine stream passing its former walls, over-
shadowed on one side by fairly high hills all richly wooded.

' Tradition says Reginald, after his father's death, sent to
Rome for a quantity of consecrated dust, and made the building commensurate with the extent to which it could be
scattered. The building was in the form of a cross. Its length
from east to west was about 136 feet by 24; and of the transept
from north to south 95 feet by 24. The south end of the transept was extended from a gable to a distance of 58 feet, and
it is thus connected another building running parallel to the

body of the church, which was crossed in its turn at the termination westward at right angles by another erection, thus giving the whole the form of a quadrangle or square. The body of the church itself, from east to west, measured 60 feet, and the height of the side walls 24 feet. In the year 1088 monks of the Cistercian order quitted the Abbey of Molesme in France, and took up their abode at Citeaux or Cistertium, a remote and desolate locality in the diocese of Chalores in Burgundy. They were called Monachi Albi, in contradistinction to the Benedictines, whose habit was entirely black, whereas the Cistercians, whilst they wore a black cowl or scapular, had all their other clothes white, as an emblem of reformation and superior purity.'[1]

An avenue leads up to this burial-place, where lie the bodies of Mackay, to whom the Bruce made a grant of the lands of Agadale; Archibald Campbell of Carradale, killed at Inverlochy; and, greatest of all, the Lord of the Isles himself, with his great two-handed sword, 'Claidheamh da Laimh,' lying sheathed by his side. There also lie abbots, monks, and warriors.

The seaward approach to the avenue is guarded by the stern old keep and outer walls of Saddell Castle, There is a good landing-place, and in the distance to the south lies the lovely island of Arran, with its majestic crags and shaggy corries—as fair a scene as the eye could dwell on or the heart of man desire.

An Act, it will be remembered, was passed in 1747 depriving all proprietors of their jurisdictions and judicial powers, and in August followed the Act against

[1] *Statistical Account of Scotland.*   W. Blackwood, 1845.

the carrying of arms. The Act against wearing the dress enforced a yet severer sentence.[1]

'In 1757 a man named M'Alpin or Drummond Macgregor was tried for alleged wearing of the forbidden Highland dress. He was acquitted on his proving that the kilt had been stitched up in the middle.

'It was in 1772 that the Duke of Montrose, then a member of the House of Commons, brought in a bill to repeal all penalties and restrictions on the Celtic garb. It passed without a dissenting voice.'

An interesting passage in the *Northern Chronicle* of December 16, 1896, regarding the regulations as to wearing the Highland dress, may here be quoted :—

'Three soldiers, who were returning to Glenshiel, after having been to Laggan for their pay, captured John M'Intosh for wearing a tartan jacket and philabeg. They determined to take him as a prisoner to Laggan, and brought him seven miles on the way hither, to within two miles of Invergarry, where they were beset by many women, who offered a guinea for the prisoner's release. The soldiers refused to take the bribe, and about twenty of the women accompanied them further on to a very thick wood, out of which six men suddenly started and pounced upon their arms before they could use them. The women joined heartily in the fray. The soldiers were disarmed, and forced to take an oath not to attempt anything against the prisoner, who was set free. When Captain Molesworth was informed of this affair, he sent out a party of sixteen men, who captured M'Intosh, "Sanders Macdonald, who was most active in the rescue, and four women who assisted in it." One of the

---

[1] '. . . should, without the alternative of a fine, be imprisoned, on the first conviction, for six months without bail, and on the second conviction be transported for seven years.'

50. TOMB AT SADDELL ABBEY.   KILTED FIGURE BROKEN IN CENTRE

... ing of arms. The Act against wearing the dress
... ... a yet severer sentence.[1]

In 1757 a man named M‘Alpin or Drummond Macgregor
was tried for alleged wearing of the forbidden Highland dress.
He was acquitted on his proving that the kilt had been stitched
up ... the centre.

It was in 1782 that the Duke of Montrose, then a member of
the House of Commons, brought in a bill to repeal all penalties
and restrictions on the Celtic garb. It passed without a dis-
sentient voice.[1]

An interesting passage in the *Northern Chronicle* of
December 16, 1885, regarding this revolt ... as ...

... and plundering. They determined
... the ... waggon, and brought her ... ...
... to ... Bridge, S... that they arrived at Invergarry, when
they were beset by many women who offered a guinea for the
prisoner's release. The soldiers refused to take the bribe, and
about twenty of the women accompanied them further on to a
very thick wood, out of which six men suddenly started and
jumped upon their arms before they could use them. The
women joined heartily in the fray. The soldiers were disarmed,
and forced to take an oath not to attempt anything against the
prisoner, who was set free. When Captain Molesworth was
informed of this affair, he sent out a party of sixteen men, who
captured M‘Intosh, Sanders Macdonald, who was most active
in the rescue, and four women who assisted in it. One of the

[1] ... should, without the alternative of a fine, be imprisoned on the first
conviction, for six months without bail, and on the second conviction be transported
for seven years.

four women arrested was afterwards, as he says, spirited by some ill-designing people to prosecute him for detaining her, and the Sheriff without notice granted a summons against him.   He denounces for misinformation "a rascally lawyer called John Shaw."   The end of this business is not told, but as the Lord Advocate took up Captain Molesworth's case, we daresay he got well out of it.

'The military officers and the civil magistrates co-operated well enough in respect to disarming and the punishment of the thieves.   Captain Molesworth, who had the misfortune of getting into trouble about the pressing for tools and horses for building the soldiers' huts with Glengarry's sanction, as well as about the arrest of the Invergarry woman, who said she was not in the mobbing, did not believe in the impartiality of Sheriff Munro, Inverness.   Yet it is pretty clear that Sheriff Munro punished people arrested for wearing the Highland dress more promptly than other Sheriffs. Sir Walter Scott represents Bailie Macwheeble wearing, after Culloden, a nightcap and morning gown which had whilom been of tartan, but which "the honest bailie had got dyed black, lest the ill-omened colour might remind his visitors of his unlucky excursion to Derby."   This was one of the many devices to which Highlanders generally resorted so as to get wearing use of their tartan clothes.   Some of the other devices were truly ludicrous.   In July 1749, the commander of the Head of Loch Rannoch, or Invercomrie, Station reports that some few Highlanders in different places make use of a short kind of trousers, different from the kilt, by which they mean to evade the law.   About the same time Captain Powell, who commanded at Inversnaid Barracks, Loch Lomond—Rob Roy's old possession,—apprehended two men for wearing the philabeg.   "But," he continues in his report, "they say it is only a woman's petticoat, tho' the only difference between the philabeg and this dress is, that this is somewhat longer and not split down before.   But to me it seems a plain evasion of the Act."   He sent his prisoners to Major Colquhoun,

who admitted them to bail until he could consult some lawyer.
Captain Scot, commander of the Braemar Castle Station, sent
a man caught wearing a plaid, with the plaid on him, to the
Sheriff of Aberdeen, who said the plaid was only a dyed
blanket, and let the man go. The sergeant sent with the
prisoner asked if people might wear their plaids if dyed?
"The Sheriff told the sergeant that the intent of the Act of
Parliament was not to oppress the poor." "I shall," says
Captain Scot, "take up all persons that I find wearing those
dyed blankets, as the Sheriff is pleased to call them." '

Special mention is made of Highland and Lowland
plaids of various kinds in the lists, made out 1685-1686,
of articles taken by the Atholl men when they raided
Argyllshire.

'The depradations. The MacGregors lifted the following
articles :—

'Item, ane new colored woman's wearing plaid, most sett to
boday red.

'Item, ane grey broken plaid, sett most to the green.

'From Peninaver they take :—

'Item, ane half playd 3 lib., and bodily apparell in all
estimated at Lib. 13, 6s. 8d.

'At Kilchattan they took from Mrs. John Duncanson, late
minister—

      Item, 1 Lowland playd mantle, etc., . . £12 0 0
      Item, 4 pair sprainged playds, . . . 46 13 4
      Item, For a Highland plaid with some oyr
            cloathes, linen and woolen, . . . 6 13 4

'In Islay, Marie Campbell, relict of umq[le] (the late) Ion
M'Caris of Donnardrie, is robbed, among other items, of—

      Item, Two pair of Truise, . . . £2 0 0
      Item, Four elnes of plaiden, ... 1 6 8
      Item, Ane small plaid at . . . . . 6 13 4 '

51. PIPERS OF 2ND SCOTS GUARDS

Now these entries prove that plaids were worn as separate garments at times, and it proves the tale of the separating of the garment to be nonsense—because the entries in this list were made before the date assigned to the so-called cutting of the Highland garb to suit the ideas of the iron-smelting Rawlinson.   At the massacre of Glencoe (1692), the brother of Acha-Triachadain asked the soldiers to allow him to be shot outside the house. To this they consented; whereupon he threw his plaid, which he had kept loose, over the faces of the firing-party, and escaped.

The price of playding (plaiding) is as follows in the 'List of Depradations in the county of Argyll, 1685-1686':—

'Item, 4 Elnes of new plading at 8s. per elne, £1, 12s.
'We also had
'Barr.
'Item, Kattearin Anderson in the tyme of the rebellion, out of fear, transported from her own house to Donald M'Fater, miller at Barr his milne, fourty elnes of linen, a pair of plaids and oyr goods to the value of £30.'

The value of the plaid is certainly put down at an uncommonly high figure, and we are left to guess if they paid as much as they charged Government.   In these lists of articles stolen we find :—

'Item, two new playds worth £24.'

The special mention of Lowland plaiding is as follows : From tenants of the MacLaines of Lochbuie :—

'Item, one Lowland playd mantle, etc., £12.'

Again, at Peninaver :—

'Item, ane half playd 3 lib., and bodily apparell, in all estimat to £13, 6s. 8d.'

The price of a pair of breeches is given in the following 'claime' :—

'Claime of goods and gear taken away from John and Donald M'Nutchesone's in Campbeltown, be Donald M'Donald, uncle to the Laird of Lergie.'

At the end, or near the end, of an immense list—

'Item, ane meet cassick and 1 pair breeches worth £8.'

We are left to guess how much was charged for the 'meet cassick.' Even if the sum be fairly divided, it is small wonder that breeches were little sought after if they cost £4 a pair!

The dress of the Marquis of Argyll, when a young man, was of black velvet and red silk stockings, as shown in a full-length portrait at Roseneath Castle. This is probably a copy from a picture in the possession of the Marquis of Lothian. When between twenty-five and thirty years of age, he dressed as cavaliers of the period did, with long Vandycked collar and cuffs, etc.

The Marquis of Argyll and his wife Margaret Douglas sent young Lord Lorne to a relative at Balloch or Taymouth ; his foster-father, writing to his tutor, considered it 'requisit he be ane discreite man, that is, ane scollar, and that can speik both Inglis and Erise, quharof I think thair may be had in Argyll.' This was written by Sir Colin Campbell of Glenurchay.

52. KILTED HIGHLANDERS
From the ' Letters from a Gentleman in the North of Scotland,' Vol. I.
Printed for S. Birt, London, 1794

53. KILTED HIGHLANDERS

From the ' Letters from a Gentleman in the North of Scotland,' Vol. II.
Printed for S. Birt, London, 1794

Archibald Campbell of Lorne's tutor appears to have worn the Highland dress, though the pupil does not seem to have done so : 'Coat and brekis to him (my Lord's sone) x quarteris of fyne skarlet, xviii. lib. the ell, xlv. lib. *Item,* ane pair of silk stockings.' And there are 'French bever hats, orange ribband points, and a Spanish pistolet for the young Lord.'

Mr. Johnne M'Len's plaid is thus mentioned :—

'*Item,* given to Mr. Johnne M'Len, pedagogue to my Lord Lorne's sone, in September 1633, ane hewit[1] plaid, pryce xii. lib.'[2]

The ancient rule of wearing the plaid should be adhered to. It is, that the plaid *is the last thing to be put on and the first to be taken off.* The army pipers set a good example in wearing the long plaid over the sword-belt, which fashion simply means that the plaid is the Highlander's greatcoat, and if needful, in wet weather, should be made to cover his arms and ornaments.

Although many works have appeared from time to time dealing with the dress of the Highlanders, very few works give actual transcripts from the original pictures or prints. It is time that a volume should appear giving contemporaneous evidence of the dress.

Typical examples of the costume of the Highlanders will be found, together with specimens of their weapons,

---

[1] The expression 'hewit' is not common, and means 'of hues or colours.'
[2] *Popular Tales of the West Highlands,* vol. iv.   J. F. Campbell of Islay.

their ornaments, and art, represented on monuments discovered on the west coast of Argyllshire. In Logan's
Gael, we read :—

'Alexander I. is represented on his seal, engraved in Dr.
Meyrick's superb work, with the fielebeag and round Targe.

'Fordun, who wrote about 1350, describes the Highlanders as
"forma spectabilis, sed amictu deformis."

'Major, who flourished in the beginning of the sixteenth
century, says, "a medio crure ad pedem caligos non habent ;
chlamyde pro veste superiore," etc.

'Lesly and Buchanan also notice it.

'Lindsay of Pitscottie, who wrote in the vulgar tongue,
cannot afford matter for the regret which some writers have
expressed, that the terms in the Latin authors are vague and
unsatisfactory. "The other pairte northerne," says he, "ar full
of mountaines, and verie rud and homelie kynd of people doeth
inhabite, which is called the Reidschankes, or wyld Scottis.
They be clothed with ane mantle, with ane schirt, faschioned
after the Irisch manner, going bair-legged to the knie."'

That the dress greatly puzzled even the Lowlanders is
proved, for Logan says :—

'The old Scots of the Low country mentioned it as "The
Highland Weed," "a light dress," etc.

'It is also evident that writers like Diodorus contented
themselves with a comparatively distant view of these strange
tribes, and was unable better to describe the dress of the Celt,
which he thought was made of cloth, ornamented in flowered
work. And Beague in 1549, from a superficial view of them,
describes the Highlanders as going almost naked, and says
they wore painted waistcoats!'[1]

'Wolfgang describes it as a small tunic that was fastened

[1] Logan, vol. i. p. 253.

54. ANCIENT HIGHLANDER

about the middle, and reached to the knees, a covering for the loins, a little cassock of various colours, covering one's nakedness.'

Now as to the breeches.

'Newte says the name for breeches in Gaelic is literally "a lock for the posteriors."   In Welsh they are termed *lhoudar*, and in Cornish, *lavrak*.

'The common name in the Highlands for this part of male attire is *briojas*, from *brioj*, restraint.

'Dr. Macpherson, who remarks that *saga* and *braccæ* were used indiscriminately by the Romans, says every Highlander in Britain knows that the *bracca* was an upper garment of divers colours. *Brat* in Gaelic is a mantle or covering, and in some parts of Scotland it is used for clothes.

'The Welsh *brati*, tattered, Camden thinks, is derived from the Celtic *braccæ*; but this does not favour the opinion that they wore trousers.

'They were used by the Getæ and other Scyths, and Pinkerton asserts that they were always the grand badge of the Goths.

'Polybius seems to prove that this part of Celtic dress was not of the form usually supposed, when he says that the Bolonians and Milanois, in the battle of Telamon, made choice of such as wore *braccæ*, being at most ease in their dress to stand the brunt of the action.

'The English breeches appear to have retained a name at first expressive of the colour, or effect, of the garment which covered the lower part of the body.   The *braccæ*, or reddish chequered tunic, was worn by all the Celts, and the *breacan* is still the national dress of their descendants, the term indicating its appearance, like the Welsh, the *Armorie*, *brech*, which signifies chequered.'

Elsewhere mention has been made by the writer of

the dress worn by the Highlanders fighting at Killiecrankie, who fought barefooted, having cast aside the
cuarans or brogues, which were made right and left.

The manufacture was as follows :—

'An oval piece of raw cow or horse's hide was drawn neatly
round the foot by thongs of the same material, by means of
holes in the margin.'[1]

During the French and American wars, hundreds of
lads came from the hills without either shoes or stockings
and enlisted.

According to Douglas's *Peerage*, James, second Earl of
Moray, was the second son of James Stewart, first Earl,
and Lady Elizabeth Stewart, who were married in 1580.

The date of the birth of the second Earl does not
appear, but he was married to Lady Anne Gordon in
1601, and died on August 6, 1638.

We have in the picture of the Earl of Moray the
evidence of the dress of the Highland noble of Charles
I.'s time. He wears the broadsword slung behind, the
dirk and the pistols—one on either side, it may be noted,—
the kilt, and very full belted plaid. The coloration of
the tartan was described by the artist, Mr. Charles Laurie,
as composed of brown and reddish colouring, as if native
dyes had been used in the manufacture of the plaiding or
in the making of the tartan.[2]

Mr. Charles Laurie saw the picture at Langton, Duns,
and made a very fine etching of the same for the work

[1] Logan, vol. i. p. 256.
[2] This picture was on view at the Grafton Street Galleries, 1895.

55. THE EARL OF MORAY

entitled the *Records of Argyll*, in which volume it will be found.

The brogues are of peculiar make, having flaps at the points of the toe which are turned over and back towards the instep, and of a tan colour. This picture was copied by the late Campbell of Islay when it was at Taymouth, in water-colours, and Islay reproduced the brogues, and habitually wore the same in the evening. They had no buckles, but had an exceedingly picturesque effect from the tan-coloured piece of leather, which was of course punctured with a pattern such as is commonly seen on Highland brogues.

The pieces of leather worn over and above such simple shoes or brogues, as above described, to protect the feet from the roughness of the heath, were called *friochan*. This was, as now, cut Vandyck fashion.

'This will be seen in the plate of the Earl of Moray, whose brogue has a turn-over piece of leather at the toe, coming over towards the instep.

'It is curious that foreigners sometimes show us what was the dress worn in Ireland and in Scotland. Magnus, king of Norway, adopted the Irish and Scottish dress, and was christened Barelegs by the Norse in consequence.

'In Elizabethan day Captain Thomas Lea wore Irish dress as worn by them when going through boggy land. This appears in the fine full-length portrait of him at Lord Dillon's house, Dythchy. He wears short trunk-hose and a cuirass, his morion under his arm, and his hand resting on his sword. Tradition has said that he was famous for his fine limbs, and before being executed by Elizabeth for complicity with the rebels, he desired these limbs to be duly recorded and preserved, as they are by this remarkable picture.　But this is not the real meaning of the extraordinary want of clothing.　It is simply that Captain Thomas Lea, having lived long in Ireland, wore the dress of the Irish of that period.　The writer well remembers this portrait being called " portrait of an Irish chief," which it is not.　In 1505 a law was passed in Parliament by which it was ordained that none should appear in that assembly (the Irish Assembly) with Irish attire, to the great discontent of the members.　Tirlogh Lenogh, chief Lord of Ulster, begged the deputy to allow him to take his chaplain in the trouse along the streets with him, because he was laughed at by everybody in his new dress.　I think it is Chaucer who relates a facetious story of these habiliments, which also tends to confirm the opinion of their not resembling modern trousers.　The Irish seem to have relinquished their ancient garb with less reluctance than might have been expected.　The Scots could not be induced to lay it aside, notwithstanding the enactments against it ; so great was their aversion to quit the dress of their fathers, that the law was ingeniously evaded, or openly contemned.'—Logan, vol. i.

Sir John Medina, in the background of his full-length portraits of Archibald, tenth Earl and first Duke of Argyll, with his two sons, John, afterwards second Duke, and Archibald, third Duke, gives a most spirited rendering of the armed Highlander of that day, kilted and armed.

Sir John, according to the fashion in vogue at that time, portrays the duke and his sons in Roman dress ; but to show that the family belonged to the Highlands he introduces Highland figures.　The armed man referred to is striding along with a large shield on his arm, and the kilt is worn short, displaying no little of the thigh.

56. THE LATE IAN CAMPBELL OF ISLAY IN HIS YOUTH, ABOUT 1840

From a Portrait lent to the Editor by MRS. CAMPBELL OF ISLAY

as they are by this remarkable picture. but this is not the
meaning of the extraordinary want of clothing. It is simply
that Captain Thomas Lea, having lived long in Ireland, wore
  a dress of the Irish of that period The writer well remembers
this portrait being called "portrait of an Irish chief," which it is
not. In 1505 a law was passed in Parliament by which it was
ordained that none should appear in that assembly (the Irish
assembly) with Irish attire, to the great discontent of the
members. Tirlough Lenough, chief Lord of Ulster, begged the
deputy to allow him to take his chaplain in the trousers long
streets with him, because he was laughed at by everybody in his
new dress. I think it is Chaucer who relates an facetious story of
these habbits which .   .   .
that not wear.   .   .   ne
nilling: these they   .   them might
have   .   and
           . so natural an evasion of the low, or rather, perhaps, it
was a Parliament to the liberty upon their scruples, or from
their aversion to quit the dress of their father that, the law
was ingeniously evaded, or openly violated as a few records.

Sir John de Fine, in the background of his full-length
portraits of Archibald, tenth Earl and first Duke of
Argyll, with his two sons, John, afterwards second
Duke and Archibald, third Duke, gives a most spirited
rendering of the armed Highlander of that day, kilted
and armed.

Sir John, according to the fashion in vogue at that
time, portrays the duke and his sons in Roman dress
but to show that the family belonged to the Highlands
he introduces Highland figures. The armed man referred
to is striding along with a large shield on his arm,
the kilt is worn short, displaying no little of the thigh.

57. THE LATE IAN CAMPBELL OF ISLAY IN HIS YOUTH

From a Daguerreotype in possession of LADY JANE DUNDAS, *née* CHARTERIS

57. THE LATE IAN CAMPBELL OF ISLAY IN HIS YOUTH

From a Daguerreotype in possession of Lady Jane Dundas, née Charteris

He wears a blue bonnet and a plume. It is a firmly drawn and admirable figure, and gives a most excellent idea of the costume of the day.

Sir John Medina was born in 1660. He died at Edinburgh in 1711. It was through the invitation of the Earl of Leven that he visited Scotland.

We can approximately name the date when this picture was painted from the faces and forms of the two boys. The elder of the two boys, who later became Duke John, would be about 14 in this picture, and he was born October 10, 1678. This places the date at which the picture was painted (1692) in the reign of King William III. We have here the dress of the Highlander at the period of the massacre of Glencoe, which took place at that date.

A very noteworthy peculiarity in this picture of Argyll painted by Medina is the broadsword at his side. The rest of the costume is Roman, but apparently Medina was at a loss to paint a Roman sword, which, it may be noted, was a short sword, and worn on the right side. Medina paints a fine broadsword with a covered guard, the broadsword which was in regular use later on, also during the '45.

Here again is a proof that the broadsword was in use before the date assigned to its use by Monsieur Demmin in his learned work on arms and armour. Argyll is wearing the fine basket-hilted broadsword on the left side, not *à la* Roman soldier. There can be no doubt at all but that this sword was painted, so to say, from life : it is drawn and painted in a masterly fashion.

There are many reasons for giving the two portraits of Ian Campbell of Islay in this work; first and foremost, because, in speaking of things Highland, it is impossible not to name Campbell of Islay. His face was of so beautiful a cast, and his form of so fine and manly a mould, and he wore his Highland dress in such a way that he was the beau-ideal of a Highlander, and it is impossible for those who ever saw him to speak of the dress of that country without recalling his singularly fine presence—when dressed in the garb of our forefathers. It is also impossible to speak of Celtic art without reference to his loving research in that field. To the day of his death, one may say, his great delight used to be to unravel, as few were capable of doing, some complicated knotted Celtic pattern which he had obtained from some lonely churchyard. His instinct was unerring in 'making out' these designs, which a lifetime of loving labours had rendered comparatively easy to him, and many a noble six-foot sheet of paper exists with his beautifully drawn out delineations of Celtic art. He was wont also to carve these patterns in alabaster. A beautiful specimen of his work is to be seen at Inveraray Castle. This he carved for the mother of the writer of these notes about the time of the Crimean War.[1]

[1] See Mr. R. C. Graham's *The Carved Stones of Islay*, page 50. James MacLehose and Sons, Glasgow, 1895.

58. EARL WILLIAM OF SUTHERLAND

From a Photo by DIXON, Golspie

59. 5TH VOLUNTEER BATTALLION ARGYLL AND SUTHERLAND HIGHLANDERS
UNDER THE COMMAND OF LIEUT.-COL CAMPBELL OF INVERNEILL

59. 5TH VOLUNTEER BATTALION ARGYLL AND SUTHERLAND HIGHLANDERS
UNDER THE COMMAND OF LIEUT.-COL. CAMPBELL OF INVERNEILL.

William, Earl of Sutherland, whose portrait is here given, was born on the 28th May 1735, and died on 16th June 1766.   The picture is by Allan Ramsay, painted in 1763, and hangs in the Hall at Dunrobin Castle.

He is represented in full Highland dress, wearing a round blue bonnet on his head, looped up on the left side.   His kilt and belted plaid are of the Sutherland tartan, his hose red, pink, and white.   The somewhat long Highland jacket is of scarlet cloth, the facings being yellow, silver-braided.   The broadsword is shown without the crimson fringe.

The officers of the Sutherland Volunteer Corps wear exactly the same dress now, theirs having been copied from the picture of Earl William, who was the seventeenth Earl.

An illustration is here given of the 5th Volunteer Battalion (Princess Louise) Argyll and Sutherland Regiment in line, at Dunoon, by Fergus and Sons of Greenock.

It was taken in 1889, and shows the regiment at a full-dress parade on broken ground.

The regiment is a typical Highland regiment, being composed of the flower of the manhood of Argyll.   The men of Cowal, Inveraray, Kilmartin, Lochgilphead and Ardrishaig, Glencoe, and Ballachulish, all contribute to the making of this fine regiment.   It is commanded by Lieut.-Colonel Campbell of Inverneill.

A passage occurs in a letter from Mr. Robert Farquharson, a chaplain in the Earl of Mar's army in 1745, which goes to show that many of the Highlanders fought in their shirts.

He says that after the battle of Killiecrankie

'there were several of the common men that died in the hills, for, having cast away their plaids at going into the battle, they had not wherewithal to cover them but their shirts ; whereas many of the gentlemen that instead of short hose did wear trewis under their belted plaids, though they were sorely pinched, did fare better in their coats and trewis than those that were naked to the belt.

' The official mention of the féileadh beag, or little kilt, occurs in the Act, passed 1747, prohibiting the wearing of the Highland dress, by which it was enacted that neither man nor boy, except such as should be employed as officers and soldiers, should on any pretence wear or put on the clothes commonly called Highland clothes—viz. the plaid, philibeg, or little kilt, trowse, shoulder-belts, or any part whatsoever of what peculiarly belongs to the Highland garb, on pain of imprisonment for six months, without the option of a fine, for the first offence, and of transportation for seven years if convicted a second time. Stewart of Garth describes the dress of the Black Watch, embodied at Taybridge in 1740: "The uniform was a scarlet jacket and waistcoat, with buff facings and white lace, tartan plaid of twelve yards, plaited round the middle of the body, the upper part being fixed on the left shoulder, ready to be thrown loose, and wrapped over both shoulders and firelock in rainy weather. At night the plaid served the purpose of a blanket, and was a sufficient covering for a Highlander. These were called belted plaids, from being kept tight to the body by a belt, and were worn on guard, reviews, and all occasions when the men were in full dress. On this belt hung the pistols when worn. In the barracks, and when not on duty, *the little kilt, or philibeg, was*

60. INVERARAY

worn, a blue bonnet with a border of white, red, and green arranged in small squares, and a tuft of feathers. The arms were a musket, a bayonet, and a large basket-hilted broadsword. These were supplied by Government. Such of the men as chose to supply themselves with pistols and dirks were allowed to carry them ; and some had targets after the fashion of the country. The sword-belt was of black leather, and the cartouche-box was carried in front, supported by a narrow belt round the middle."[1]

Now, in the plate of Inveraray given in this volume, the two figures in the foreground wear, the one on the reader's left hand the small kilt or ' féileadh beag,' and the figure on the right the full-dress belted plaid with a tuft of feathers in the blue bonnet.

The plate of old Inveraray Castle and market-place is of interest for more reasons than one. Firstly, it is the work of the engineer who worked under the directions of the Duke of Cumberland, and the accuracy of various points given has been proved by those who know every inch of the ground.

Secondly, it contains groups of people walking about dressed in the Highland dress, and also shows the ordinary English dress of that period.

Thirdly, it shows the old Castle as Queen Mary saw it when she hunted the deer for three days at Inveraray, and the building as it existed prior to her time, and as known to the Marquis of Argyll and his son, both of whom were beheaded, and as known to the first, second, and third Dukes of Argyll. This is the building which

[1] *Records of Argyll.* Blackwood and Sons.

became the headquarters of the Atholl chief and his men when they laid waste the district of Cowal, etc., and where the immortal Dugald Dalgetty sojourned for a while according to the *Legend of Montrose.*

The kilt has been worn at various lengths. In the days of Charles I. it was worn very short, showing the whole of the knee and a portion of the leg above the same. It was also worn short in 1745. When the kilt has been adjusted, the wearer kneeling, it should barely touch the ground. A kilt is better worn short, as it is apt to look ill and give a kick that is very ugly in walking if worn too long. It should hang from the hip, swinging freely to the motion of the body.

The amount of stuff varies with the wearer and the thickness of the tartan or cloth. Many take seven and a half to eight yards to make a full and handsome kilt. Nothing looks worse than one made of too little material. The same applies to the shoulder-plaid, which should be, what it originally was, large and ample enough to cover the body when raining or cold.

The London-Scottish Rifle Volunteers set the War Office an excellent example as to this, and wear a useful and full plaid. The authorities are too apt to deal out tartan insufficient to clothe the troops handsomely, and the shoulder-plaid becomes simply an ornament, not an article of dress conducing to the comfort of the men. The stinting of the tartan is unworthy of the country, and a grotesque form of economising.

To his Grace the DUK
And Old Castle of INVERARAY fro
Most

GYLE This Prospect of Duniquich

Place is Most humbly Inscribd by his Grace's

most Servant, Paul Sandby.

In some of the Highland regiments the 'box-pleat' is in use for the kilt, but it is a troublesome style of pleating to keep in perfect order.   The tendency of this form of pleating is to get sooner out of shape than the other and simpler way usually adopted.   The swing of the garment tends at once to displace the arrangement and broaden out each pleat, and this mode of making up the dress needs more constant attention and repair than the other and simpler forms.   It does not stand so well, though it looks handsome when first turned out by the regimental tailor.

The following account of Prince Charlie, when close to Portree, Skye, in a famished condition, and wet through, is given.   Those who were with the Prince, Donald Roy and Malcolm MacLeod and Flora MacDonald, went to an inn :—

'The Prince called for a dram in the first place, of which he seemed much in need, as the rain was streaming down his plaid, and he had no trews or philibeg.   The company joined in urging him to shift and put on a dry shirt, Donald Roy offering him his philibeg.   He at first refused, from delicacy towards Miss MacDonald; but he was at length prevailed on to disregard ceremony. . . . As there was no fermented liquor in Skye, the Prince had to drink out of a rough-looking wooden vessel, used by the landlord to bale his boat. . . . Charles then put it to his lips and took a hearty draught, after which he put on his philibeg and other clothes.'

We have here the special mention of the dripping plaid he had as a separate article of dress, and of the *philibeg* or *little kilt* as a *separate article of dress also*.

This account is given in the *History of the Rebellion of* 1745-6, by Robert Chambers, and is taken from authentic documents.

Mr. George P. Johnston, of No. 33 George Street, Edinburgh, sent to the writer of these notes on dress a curious plate showing two kilted mariners, dated 1693. The tartan lines are here clearly shown. It also is an illustration of the use of 'the little kilt.' There is no indication here of the use of the plaid. The head-dress shows the sailor's cap of that period; the emblems in the hands of the figures also show that these are intended for mariners of the period.

62. *From a painting, dated 1750, in Armadale Castle.*

CHAPTER XII

CONCERNING HIGHLAND DRESS—*continued*

IN this work the writer does not propose to go into the history of tartan, for that has been done in a previous volume, and has, since 1885—when the *Records of Argyll* appeared—been further dealt with by others. It will here be sufficient to recall that 'when King James v. made a hunting expedition into the Highlands in 1538, a Highland dress was provided for the occasion,' and the accounts of the Lord High Treasurer show that it consisted of a 'Short Heland Coit,' hose of 'tertane,' and a syde—*i.e.* an unusually long shirt.

Buchanan, writing in 1582, states that the colours preferred for the stripes of the variegated stuffs that the Highlanders used for clothing were chiefly purple and blue; but the diversely coloured fabrics which had been formerly common were then falling into disuse, and the common people had mostly brown garments—of the colour of the heather, in order that when they lay among the heather, the bright colours of their clothing might not betray them.

This leads the writer to go back to the portrait of the

Earl of Moray, given in this work. The general coloration of the tartan is a beautiful rich brown or reddish brown colour.

Mr. J. Dransfield reminds us of the following notes on hunting, and the costume described by Taylor, the Water-Poet.

Taylor, the Water-Poet, about 1630 to 1640 visited the Highlands of Scotland, and gives an account of the mode in which huntings were conducted there in the seventeenth century, having been present on such an occasion :—

'There did I find the truly noble and right hon. lords John Erskine, Earl of Mar ; James Stuart, Earl of Murray ; George Gordon, Earl of Engye, son and heir to the Marquis of Huntley ; James Erskine, Earl of Buchan ; and John, Lord Erskine, son and heir to the Earl of Mar ; and their countesses, with my much honored and my last assured and approved friend Sir William Murray, knight of Abercarney, and hundreds of others, knights, squires, and their followers, all and every man in general in one habit, as if Lycurgus had been there and made laws of equality. For once in the year, which is the whole month of August and sometimes part of September, many of the nobility and gentry of the kingdom (for their pleasure) do come into these Highland counties to hunt, when they do conform them-selves to the habit of Highlandmen, who for the most part speak nothing but Irish, and in former times were those people which were called the Red-Shanks. Their habit is shoes with but one sole a-piece, stockings (which they call short hose) made of a warm stuff of divers colours which they call tartan ; as for breeches many of them nor their forefathers never wore any but a jerkin of the same stuff that their hose is made of, their garters being bands or wreaths of hay or straw, with a plaid about their shoulders, which is a mantle of divers colours, much finer and

63. PRIVATE OF PRINCESS LOUISE'S ARGYLL AND SUTHERLAND HIGHLANDERS

Photograph by Mr. Louis, Euston Road, London

Plaid of Money given in this work The general
coloration the tartan is a beautiful rich or or
reddish brown colour.

Mr. Dransfield reminds us of the following notes
on hunting, and the costume described by Taylor, the
Water-Poet.

Taylor, the Water-Poet, about 1630 to 1640 visited the
Highlands of Scotland, and gives an account of the mode
in which huntings were conducted there in the seventeenth
century, having been present on such an occasion :—

"There did I see the truly noble and right honourable Lord
Enzie, son of the Earl of Huntley, and Lord Murray, son

94. PLAID OF PRINCESS LOUISE'S ARGYLL AND SUTHERLAND HIGHLANDERS

Photograph by Mr. Lorio, Euston Road, London

 to the Earl of Tullibardine, and
diverse others, to get to their lodging, and in divers others,
who were agreed, and their men were all ready, and in general
in one habit, as if Lycurgus had been there and made laws of
apparel. For once in the year, which is the whole month of
August and sometimes part of September, many of the nobility
and gentry of the kingdom (for their pleasure) do come into
these Highland counties to hunt, where they do conform themselves to the habit of Highlandmen, who for the most part
nothing but Irish, and in former times were those people which
were called the Red-Shanks. Their habit is shoes with but one
sole a-piece, stockings (which they call short hose) made of a
warm stuff of divers colours which they call tartan; as for
breeches many of them nor their forefathers never wore any but
a jerkin of the same stuff that their hose is made of, their garters
being bands or wreaths of hay or straw, with a plaid about their
shoulders, which is a mantle of divers colours, much finer and

ML.794

lighter stuff than their hose, with blue flat caps on their heads, a
handkerchief knit with two knots about their necks, and thus
are they attired.   Now their weapons are long bows and forked
arrows, swords and targets, harquebusses, muskets, dirks, and
Lochaber axes.   With these arms I found many of them armed
for the hunting.   As for their attire, any man of what degree, or
even that comes amongst them, must not disdain to wear it, for
if they do then they will disdain tó hunt or willingly to bring in
their dogs: but if men be bound unto them and be in their
habit, then are they conquered with kindness, and the sport will
be plentiful.   This was the reason that I found so many noble-
men and gentlemen in those shapes.'

The account Taylor also gives of the hunting is very
amusing.   And now, referring to Sir Thomas Wortley,
one of the old Masters of Penistone Harriers, I read :—

'Adverting to Sir Thomas Wortley of Wortley, the represent-
ative of an ancient Yorkshire family, who was an eminent
personage in his time, and knight of the body of four successive
sovereigns, Edward IV., Richard III., Henry VII., and Henry VIII.,
an old illuminated pedigree, after referring to the "good service"
Sir Thomas did "in the warres," thus proceeds to speak of his
recreation : "First he was much given to shootinge in the long
bow, and many of his men were cunninge archers, and in them
he did much delite.   Also he had much delite in huntinge, that
he did builde in the middest of his forest of Wharncliffe a
house or lodge, at which house he did lye for most part of the
grouse tyme; and the worshipfull of the countrye did ther
resorte unto hime, havinge ther with hime pastime and good
cheare.   Many tymes he would go into the Forest of the Peake
and set up ther his tent, with great provision of vitales, havinge
in his company many worshipfull persons, with his own family,
and would remain ther seven weeks or more, hunting and making
other costly pastimes unto his companye.   Sir Thomas had

such a kinde and brede of hounds, and their cunninge in huntinge it was such that the fame of them went into Scotland, so that the Kinge of Scots did write his letters desieringe hime to have some of his houndes ; at which request he did send him ten copple with his owne huntsman, which did remaine there eleven whole years."'

The learned Mr. William F. Skene, whose acquaintance the writer made when a boy in 1858, says that 'it has likewise been doubted whether the distinction of Clan Tartans was known at that period' (he is speaking of A.D. 1538); but Martin seems to set that question at rest, for in his valuable account of the Western Isles, he says : 'Every Isle differs from each other in their fancy of making plaids, as to the stripes, or breadth, or colours.' Now this difference is so great throughout the mainland of the Highlands, that persons who have seen those places are able, at the first view of a man's plaid, to guess the place of his residence. It was many years later than the date of the publication of Mr. Skene's book that the Culloden incident, painted by D. Morier for the Duke of Cumberland, was exhibited, to the delight of those who knew of the wearing of the tartan anterior to, and at the time of, the 1745. This picture, exhibited by Her Majesty the Queen at the Naval and Military Exhibition at Chelsea, proved the point.

It has elsewhere been proved by the writer that Campbell of Lochnell and Ardslignish, fighting on Prince Charlie's side, wore the common dark Clan Campbell tartan at the battle, and we are expressly

INCIDENT IN THE SC

TCH REBELLION, 1745.

told that the royal troops had trouble to distinguish Campbells from those fighting on Prince Charlie's side. The Campbells, like others, wore their clan colours at the battle, whether Jacobite or on the side of King George. The only way the Government troops could distinguish friend from foe was by the white or black cockade—some wore a red cockade fighting on the Hanoverian side, it is said,—and we are told of one case where a man had lost his cap, and was about to be cut down in the pursuit, when he called out that he was a Campbell. Confusion arose also where the white cockade had become black with use, and the smoke and grime of the battle.

Of course many knew that tartan was worn in Montrose's day, or suspected this; but it was hard to prove till attested to in our day by Dr. Alexander Stewart, better known as Nether Lochaber, who saw a 'swatch' cut from the plaid of a fallen Jacobite at Kilsyth who was one of the Stewart clan. It was of Stewart clan-tartan.

The tartan relic from Kilsyth had a double interest, for it contained in its folds the charm-stone which the fallen clansman had worn. These charm-stones were always sacred things to the Highlander.

The battle incident painted for the Duke of Cumberland proves that a variety of clan-tartans were worn, and the mode in which the jacket is cut from the tartan web —on the bias—proves the picture was painted from the living model, and from actual Highland jackets. No Englishman or foreigner would have known how these jackets were cut and shaped. We have here the best internal evidence possible.

The photograph of the battle-piece from the original picture of the incident in the Rebellion, 1745, was taken when that picture was on exhibition at Chelsea, permission to have the same copied having been graciously granted by Her Majesty the Queen. Mr. Ernest Griset copied the picture in oils, and this copy was reproduced by Messrs. W. and A. K. Johnstone in a coloured lithograph which forms the frontispiece of a pamphlet published by them, called *The Children of the Mist*. This Plate shows the various specimens of tartans painted by D. Morier, who depicted the uniforms of the army commanded by the Duke of Cumberland. It is of deep interest to all Highlanders and lovers of costume, as he painted every detail belonging to the uniforms both of the officers, non-commissioned officers, and men. The picture of the Grenadier of the 42nd Regiment, also painted by D. Morier, shows the red stripe which runs through the dark Atholl tartan. This is an excellent proof of the accuracy of this artist, as one company of the Black Watch wore the Atholl tartan. This is specially mentioned in Stewart's book, a work thoroughly reliable for accuracy of detail. The Highland soldiers must have been painted from prisoners, as it is impossible that an English soldier, sitting as

65. GRENADIER OF THE 42ND REGIMENT, A.D. 1745

65. GRENADIER OF THE 42ND REGIMENT, A.D. 1745

... ... Highland jackets
... ... would have known how ...
... ... We have here the ...
... ...

... photograph of the ... ... in the original
... the world at in the Rebellion 1745, ...
... ... an exhibition at Chelsea premises
... ... the same copied having been ... ...
granted by Her Majesty the Queen. Mr. ... ...
... the plates In other ... ...
by Messrs. W ... ...
lithograph which ... ...
published by ...
The ... ...
painted by ... ... the ...
the ... recommend by the Duke of Cumberland
of ... ... all Highlanders ...
... ... painted every detail ... ...
... ... of ... ...
... ... 42
... show the ...
... Atholl ...
... of the ... ...
... the Atholl ...
... ... book, a ...
... of ... The ...
... from prints
English soldier ...

a model, could have put on the Highland dress so well. It is certain that the Duke of Cumberland had not only the true dresses worn on the battlefield, but also the living model for Morier to paint from when he placed this record on canvas.

The home of these military pictures is Windsor Castle. It was here that the late Campbell of Islay saw the picture of the 42nd Grenadier, for he writes concerning the Atholl red stripe in the tartan in a letter addressed to the writer of this book.

The date of Campbell of Islay's letter is 1871, written shortly before the marriage of Lord Lorne with H.R.H. the Princess Louise. The following account of D. Morier is taken from Bryan's *Dictionary of Painters and Engravers.*

'MORIER, DAVID.—This artist was born at Berne, in Switzerland, about the year 1705. He came to England soon after the battle of Dettingen, and was presented to the Duke of Cumberland by Sir Edward Faulkener, who settled on him a pension of two hundred pounds a year. He distinguished himself as a painter of battles, managed horses, etc., and also painted portraits, in which he was extensively employed. He died in 1770, and was buried in St. James's, Clerkenwell.'

He was, according to this, forty years of age at the time of the '45, and would have been in his prime an experienced artist in costume and detail of arms. No more conclusive proof of distinctive clan colours has been exhibited, and it silences all dispute on the question at once and for all time.

A memorandum may here be given of the arms

secured after the battle of Culloden (*History of the Rebellion of* 1745, p. 311):—

'The Duke of Cumberland employed the few days immediately following the battle [of Culloden] in securing and disposing of the spoil, which was very considerable. He had taken 30 pieces of cannon, 2320 firelocks, 190 broadswords, 37 barrels of powder, and 22 carts of ammunition. The soldiers were allowed half a crown for every musket, and a shilling for every broadsword which they could bring into quarters; it being the anxious wish of Government to keep as many arms as possible out of the hands of the natives. In order, moreover, to put a great public indignity upon the insurgents, the sum of sixteen guineas was allowed for each stand of their colours; and fourteen of these melancholy emblems of departed glory being thus procured, they were, on the 4th of June, carried by a procession of chimney-sweeps from the Castle to the Cross of Edinburgh, and there burned by the hands of the common hangman, with many marks of contempt.

'The victory of Culloden was cheaply purchased by the British army. The whole amount of killed, wounded, and missing was 310, including few officers, and but one man of distinction. This last was Lord Robert Kerr, second son of the Marquis of Lothian, a captain of grenadiers in Barrel's regiment. Standing at the head of his company when the Highlanders made the charge, he received the first man upon his spontoon, but was instantly slain with many wounds.'

The question may be asked: What proofs are there of distinctive clan-tartans having been in use prior to the formation of Highland regiments? The Black Watch when first raised wore the distinctive clan-tartan

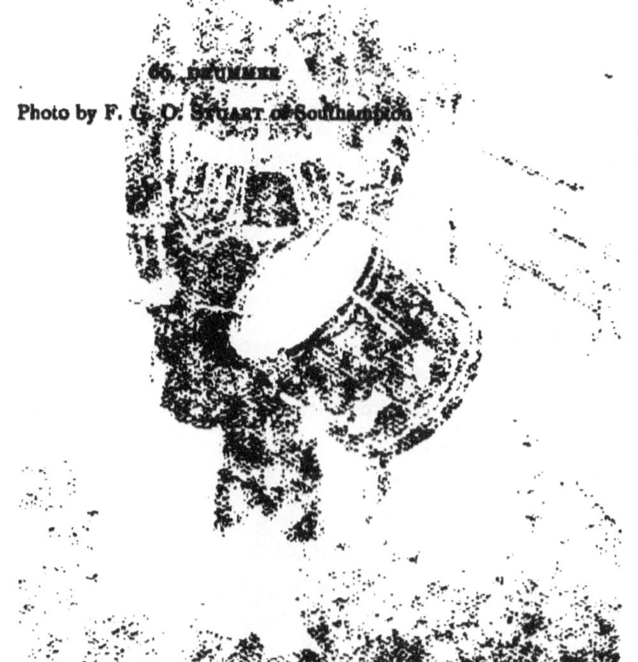

66. DRUMMER
Photo by F. G. O. Stuart of Southampton

secured after the battle of Culloden (*History of the Rebellion of 1745, p. 311*):—

'The Duke of Cumberland employed the few days immediately following the battle [of Culloden] in securing and disposing of the spoil, which was very considerable. He had taken 30 pieces of cannon, 2320 firelocks, 190 broadswords, 37 barrels of powder, and a quantity of ammunition. The soldiers were allowed half a crown for every musket, and a shilling for every broadsword which they could bring into quarters; it being the anxious wish of Government to keep as many arms as possible out of the hands of the natives. In order, moreover, to put a stop to private ... upon his own safety, the sum of seven guineas ... ... free ... ... fourteen ... ...

... ...

... ...

... hands of the ... ...

'The victory at Culloden was cheaply purchased by the British army. The whole amount of killed, wounded, missing was 310, including few officers, and but one man of distinction. This last was Lord Robert Kerr, second son of the Marquis of Lothian, a captain of grenadiers in Barrell's regiment. Standing at the head of his company when the Highlanders made the charge, he received the first man upon his spontoon, but was instantly slain with many wounds.'

The question may be asked: What proofs are there of distinctive clan tartans having been in use prior to the formation of Highland regiments? The Black Watch when first raised wore the distinctive clan-tartan

of its various leaders, and when this force became regimented, and no longer acted as independent companies, Lord Crawford, being a Lowlander, decided that a new set of tartan be adopted. This was to avoid bickerings and refusals of one company, or several companies, to adopt a tartan not that of their particular leader. When the 43rd—or as it was later called, 42nd—were first raised, they wore a sett peculiar to no clan.

If Grose is correct in his *Military Antiquities*, the set as shown in his plates is decidedly peculiar.

The Black Watch was originally composed of six companies; three, distinguished by the name of large companies, consisted of one hundred men each, and three smaller companies of seventy men each. The commissions of the officers were dated in October and the following months of 1739. The men were not assembled until the month of May 1740; the whole were then mustered in a field between Tay Bridge and Aberfeldy.

The clan-tartans represented were those of Lord Lovat, Sir Duncan Campbell of Lochnell, and Colonel Grant of Ballindalloch, who were granted captain's commissions and three companies of seventy-five men each, of which Colonel Alexander Campbell of Finab, John Campbell of Carrick, and George Munro of Culcairn were appointed Captain-Lieutenants.

In mentioning Lochnell, it will be well here to state

that the Jacobite Campbell of Ardslignish of the 1745 wore Campbell tartan at the battle of Culloden, and that his plaid, worn on the field of battle, was constantly seen in the hands of the late Mrs. Lilias Davidson, *née* Miss Campbell of Lochnell and Ardslignish.

The following is what this lady wrote :—

BUSHEY PARK, TEDDINGTON,
January 1882.

'I HAVE received your letter with much pleasure, and hasten to say that my sister and I have never heard of any tartan being worn by the Lochnells except the plain Campbell, composed exclusively of black, blue, and green. We had the plaid which was worn by my great-grandfather (Alexander Campbell of Ardslignish) at the battle of Culloden ; it was what is called the 42nd, and of a dark sombre colour. Possibly, however, time, which has since destroyed, might in our day have affected any brightness it may originally have possessed. Perhaps I should say this, that this Ardslignish was Sir Duncan Campbell of Lochnell's brother. My impression, derived from my father, the ninth Lochnell, is, that the old clan-tartan was very dark, even in its greens and blues.'

Now we come to a detail connected with the Atholl tartan which is of value, as it shows what Atholl clan-tartan was, how Lord John Murray introduced it into the Grenadier company, which was, of course, the right-hand company, and although this company had to wear the high-peaked cap of the Georgian troops, how jealously Lord John Murray guarded the tartan and gave it to this company.

The red line does not show in the plate, but the

67. GROUP OF THREE MEN OF THE QUEEN'S OWN CAMERON HIGHLANDERS,
THE OLD 79TH

Photo by Messrs. WILSON of Aberdeen

DR. TULLOCH PIPE OF THE 42 BLACK WATCH GORDON HIGHLANDERS
...ng reg. 79th.

Photo by Reeves, Watson in Aberdeen.

...d

of ... ... impression, derived fr...
th... ... ... is ... the old clan-tartan w
even in its greens and blues."

Now we come to a detail connected with
tartan which is of value, as it shows v
clan-tartan was, how Lord John Murray ir
into the Grenadier company, which was, of
right-hand company, and although this co
to wear the high-peaked cap of the Gr...
how jealously Lord John Murray guarded
and gave it to this company.

The red line does not show in the r'

QUEEN'S OWN CAMERON HIGHLANDERS 10,555

artist, D. Morier, gives it with great minuteness in his original oil-painting.

This painting was unknown to the writer in 1882 and in 1885, when Messrs. Blackwood published his *Records of Argyll.*

Here is what Stewart says of the Atholl tartan, which proves what was asserted previously :—

'While the companies acted independently, each commander assumed the tartan of his own clan, when embodied ; no clan having a superior claim to offer a uniform plaid to the whole, and Lord Crawford, the colonel, being a Lowlander, a new pattern was assumed, and which has ever since been known as the 42nd or Black Watch tartan, being distinct from all others. Lord John Murray gave the Atholl tartan for the philibeg. The difference was only a stripe of scarlet to distinguish it from that of the belted plaid.'

Now this statement alone shows the kilt was separate from the belted plaid in the 42nd.

The doubt cast on the antiquity of the tartan not being older than the regiments is a very foolish doubt, as the taking of a hitherto unknown sett is the proof that clan-tartans were universal, and that distinctive clan-tartan existed, and such distinctions were jealously kept up. If any further proof be needed, the following statement by the Rev. Dr. Alexander Stewart will be useful :—

'There is no doubt at all that distinctive clan-tartans were worn so long ago at least as 1645, and probably at a much earlier date.

'In 1853, thirty years ago, I saw a leng or clach-bhuaidh, a rock crystal amulet, of pigeon-egg shape and size, set in silver, and attached to a good long silver chain of massive links. It was kept carefully stowed away in the under " shottle " of a massive fir-wood chest or ciste (kist), one of those much-valued articles of family furniture that descended from father to son, and from mother to daughter. It was wrapped up in a small square of MacKenzie[1] tartan about the size of a lady's pocket handkerchief. The great-great-grandfather of the owner of the talisman was "out" with Montrose. He carried this talisman about his person for good luck generally, but mainly because of his belief that while he had it about him he was perfectly safe from wounds and death. He was, however, killed at Kilsyth ; and when his body was buried on or near the field of battle, the much-prized talisman was taken from his person, *and wrapped in a piece torn from his bloodstained plaid*, and thus religiously preserved and carried back by one of his companions to his sorrowing friends at Nether Lochaber. You know the feeling of Highlanders on these matters. Both talisman and the tartan in which it was carefully wrapped up were exactly in the same state as when they reached Lochaber from Kilsyth some two hundred and odd years previously.'

Yet further proof is given by Dr. Alexander Stewart, who says :—

'About the same time (1853), or shortly afterwards, I saw a copy of the Bible—the Latin Vulgate—in the possession of my friend the late Charles Stewart of Acha-nan-con in Appin. It was bound in vellum, and the vellum itself was covered with a closely stitched outer cover of Stewart tartan. It had at one time belonged to the Stewarts of Invernehyle (Inbhir-na-h-aighle). On a fly-leaf was an inscription, saying that the

---

[1] In the pamphlet *Children of the Mist* read MacKenzie Tartan instead of Stewart. —A. C. Ed.

68. PIPE-MAJOR ROBB, FORMERLY OF THE 93RD SUTHERLAND HIGHLANDERS

Photo by F. G. O. STUART of Southampton

[illegible]

[illegible] years ago, [illegible] long [illegible] chain and
[illegible] pigeon, shape and size, [illegible]
[illegible] good long silver chain or massiv[e]
[illegible] shoulder [illegible]
[illegible] on one [illegible] of those [illegible]
[illegible] Scotland, this [illegible] from [illegible]
[illegible] daughter. It was a pretty
[illegible]
[illegible] The great grand-father of the [illegible]
[illegible] with Monroe. He married this
[illegible] on his pasture for g[illegible] dark grey [illegible]
[illegible] called [illegible] he [illegible]
[illegible]
[illegible]

[illegible] G. O. Stuart, of Southampton [illegible]

[illegible]

[illegible]

[illegible]

[illegible] Stewart
who [illegible]

[illegible] towards [illegible] saw
[illegible] the person of
my friend [illegible] son is appai[illegible]
[illegible] was covered with
[illegible] cover of [illegible] It had
[illegible]
[illegible]

[illegible] Michael [illegible]

volume had been *so found* by Helen Campbell of Dunstaffnage, spouse of Duncan Stewart of Invernehyle, and *the date* 1639. This volume is probably still in existence.'

King Charles II.'s marriage coat, preserved among the curiosities at Bestwood, Notts, is ornamented with ribbons of Royal Stewart tartan now much faded. The Duchess of St. Albans describes the coat in a letter to Lady Millais, the widow of Sir John E. Millais, *P*.R.A.

In the 'Battle Incident—Culloden,' painted by D. Morier for the Duke of Cumberland, there are many varieties of tartan depicted.

In *Waifs and Strays of Celtic Tradition*, see 'The Black Raven of Glengarry,' vol. v. pp. 63, 64. The youngest son of Glengarry—the two elder ones were killed—was called the Black Raven of Glengarry. Glengarry tells his son that an insulting message has been received from Kintail about a boundary-line. The son says, 'My two brothers were killed in your foolish quarrels, and if there must be fighting for so foolish a cause, you must do it yourself.' The father starts off to settle the dispute; but the Raven, or third son, when they were out of sight, puts on his best suit of armour, takes several turns round the hill to elude the notice of any straggler, and sets off with utmost speed to get ahead of his father. Before evening he reaches the head of Loch Duich. Next day he procures a plaid of MacKenzie tartan, which he wraps round him to disguise the red badge (*suaicheautes dearg*) of Glengarry, and makes his way to the headquarters of the enemy at Donan Isle, where the Kintail men were rapidly gathering to the fray. It was the custom to set a long board out supplied with abundance of food (*bòrd mòr fada*) for the entertainment of those assembled. The chief sat at the head, and every man on taking his place stuck his dirk in the edge of the table in front of him before sitting down.

The Black Raven got in unnoticed, from his plaid concealing his badge. He says to the man next him that he wants to sit next Kintail. On taking his seat he threw Kintail backwards on the ground, and placed his foot on him to keep him down, the point of his dirk resting on the prostrate man's breast. His plaid having slipped aside, the red (*an dearg*) was exposed, and in an instant a hundred dirks were ready to riddle him. But he said, 'The moment I am approached, your chief is a dead man!' He then made Kintail take an oath that no further hostilities should henceforth take place. The son met the father, and told him peace was concluded, and how it was brought about.

This is a very remarkable mention of clan-tartan, and dates back at least as early as the Montrose wars, as pointed out in a leader in the *Daily News*, dated April 5, 1895.

The sporran should not be so large that it hides the beauty of the kilt, and very heavy mounts on it

1. Brass top, doe-skin pouch, secret fastening, fine whorl knob, probably early seventeenth century.

2 and 3. Full dress sporrans, brass topped, eight tassels each, secret spring fastenings.

4. Square-topped brass sporran, with secret spring, very ancient pattern, seal-skin pouch.

5. Ancient sporran, brass topped, with secret catches or springs, doe-skin pouch.

6. Sporran top, square-shaped, from Culloden Moor, found by a keeper named Ross while shooting.

...and [illegible] the real badge (*suaicheantas dearg*)
of Cintagery, and made his way to the headquarters of
the enemy of [illegible] Isle, where the Kintail men were
rapidly [illegible] to the fray. It was the custom to
set a long board out supplied with abundance of food
(*biadh a's [illegible]*) for the entertainment of those assembled.
The chief sat at the head, and every man [illegible] taking
his place stuck his dirk in the edge of the table [illegible]
a bit before sitting down.

[illegible]

[illegible] he said, "I or sooner if you approach
your chief is a dead man." He then made Kintail take
an oath that no further hostilities should [illegible] with [illegible]
[illegible]. The son met the father, and told him peace was
concluded, and thus it was brought about.

This is a very remarkable mention of clan-tartan, and
goes back at least as early as the Montrose wars, as
pointed out in a leader in the *Daily News*, dated April
5, 1895.

The sporran should not be so large that it hides the
beauty of the kilt, and very heavy [illegible] one of [illegible]

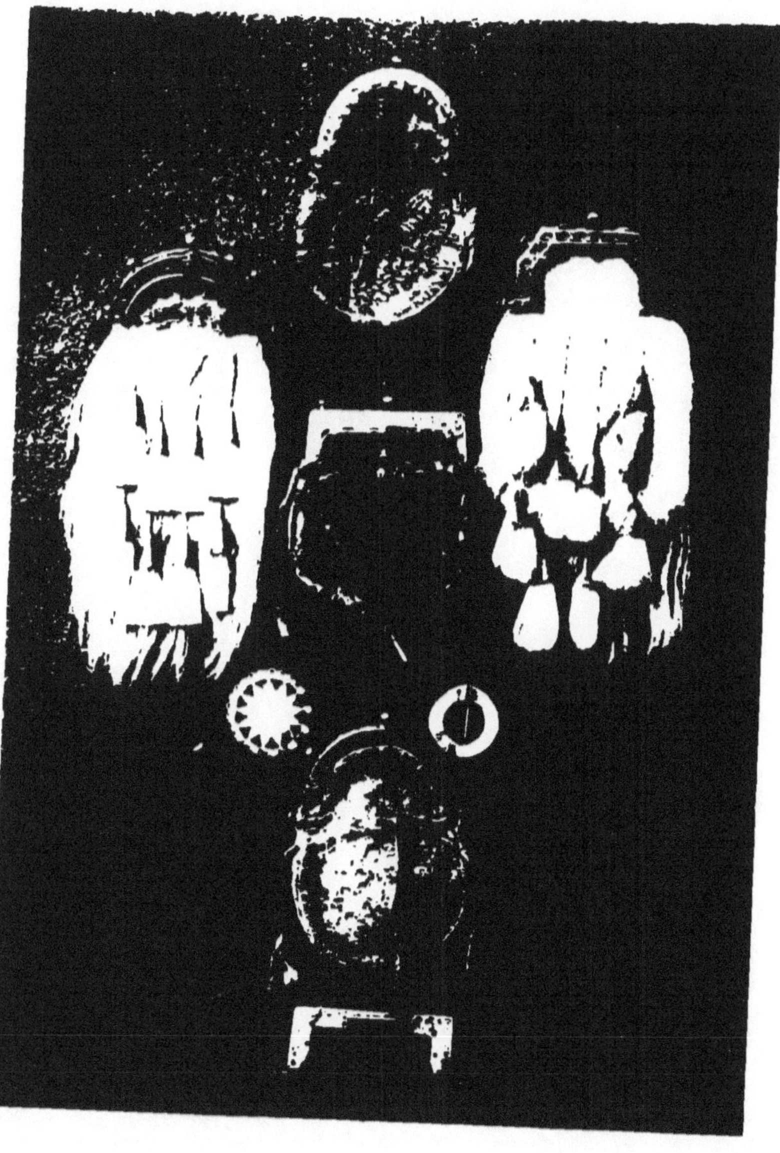

look bad.   The large sporrans were in vogue some forty years ago or so, and are not of the ancient form or style, as will be seen by examples given in this volume.

The Glengarry requires very careful selecting.   Each individual must study what suits him best, whether the high-cocked Glengarry, or the shape much in vogue in the Highland regiments, which is cut low.   The bonnet should be cocked on the right side of the head, and just touching the right ear.

The bonnets made in the early years of Walter Scott, as shown in the engravings of various chiefs who were present in Edinburgh during the visit to that town of King George IV., show that a high Glengarry was much in vogue.   It would seem to have got cut down a good deal since that period.

The broad bonnet shown in the portrait of the Earl of Moray is of true Highland shape; that worn by the Black Watch was also round, being cocked up on the left side—pinned up or looped up, with the cockade showing well to the front.

The very broad thrum bonnet was in use in the Low-lands.

Those who have a right to the eagle plume in the bonnet are the following :—

A chief of a clan wears three eagle's feathers.

A chieftain, or sons of the chief, two feathers.

The gentry, a solitary plume.

The garter in ancient days was worn well to the outer

side of the leg, not to the front, as in the case of some of
the regiments.   This is shown by a picture at Taymouth
Castle, and in the portrait of the Earl of Moray, and by
other evidence.

The belted plaid should not be worn too long, but it
should come below the kilt.

The long plaid, also, should not be worn, as is often
the case, almost touching the ankle, and at times the
fringe almost on the ground.   The fringe ought never to
come lower than the middle of the calf.   Nothing looks
more untidy than to see the long plaid's fringed ends
almost sweeping the ground.   It could not thus be worn
when walking over the heather or through brushwood,
and the dress of a Highlander should be of such a nature
that it could be worn on the mountain or at Court.

Mr. Alexander Carmichael, the learned collector of
Hebridean hymns, published a short time ago some
valuable notes on pampooties, or shoes of raw hide.   It
will be best to quote some of the letters sent on this
subject to Mr. Carmichael. [1]

'VICTORIA SQUARE,
'STIRLING, February 7, 1894.

'MY DEAR SHERIFF MACKAY,—The making of Highland "Brogues,"
although universal in the Scottish Highlands a century ago, and for
centuries previous, is now all but a lost art.   Of course I do not refer to the
fashionable shoe which goes by that name, and resembles the original
brogue only in the cut of the uppers, with double and winged frochans
(toecaps), double quarters, and vandyked edges.   In Sinclair's *Statistical
Account* (now nearly 100 years old) several parishes are mentioned as
having so many *brogue* makers and so many *shoe* makers.   That may
serve to mark the time when the simple but ingenious and tasteful art of the

---

[1] *Proceedings* of the Society of Antiquaries of Scotland.

70. SAMUEL M‘PHERSON AT BAYONET EXERCISE

From a Drawing by CRUIKSHANK

former began to be superseded by the more complicated and varied styles of the latter.

'In Balquidder, Perthshire, a family of M'Diarmids has been first *brogue* and then *shoe* makers for generations. The present descendant, Duncan M'Diarmid, still possesses the art of broguemaker, and probably there is not another man who does so within sight of Stirling Castle.

'Duncan is getting old, and has no son who is likely to take up his business, so I asked him to make a pair of genuine Highland brogues for me, that they might be put into our local museum before the art of making such articles becomes quite extinct in our district.

'That is the pair I have borrowed and sent to you now. I asked the curator to wear them in the Museum for a few weeks to take off the bran-new appearance, and I see he has done so. You may remark about them—

'1st. The uppers are of deer-skin, tanned and dressed, and the sole of light bullock's hide. They are brogues for house wear; those for outdoor wear would be precisely the same for " make," but of thicker materials.

'2nd. They are sewed with a single lace. The ancient broguemaker did not understand the modern art of sewing with double rosin ends.

'3rd. The sewing is entirely done with a *leather lace* both in the sole and upper parts. No hemp, lint, linen, or silk thread was used by Highlanders in making their foot coverings. Indeed, there was nothing besides the *leather* they made used for brogues except the *wooden pins*, which the craftsman made for himself (now all made by Yankee machinery and imported from America) and used at the heels; and the buckle, which was often ornate, and of valuable metal.

'4th. When I got the shoes from M'Diarmid a month or two ago, he said these were "made precisely the same as the shoes Prince Charlie wore." Of course I cannot certify this to be true, but probably it is so.—Yours sincerely,   R. YELLOWLEES.

'It may be hoped that the art of brogue-making will not, as Mr. Yellowlees fears, entirely die out. It would certainly be curious if the more ancient *Cuaran* survived the *Brogue*, and the Cuaran is still, beyond doubt, made and worn by a considerable number of Irish and Scotch islanders. Sir Arthur Mitchell, in his work *The Past in the Present*, mentions, with reference to the Scottish *Rivelin*, " There is probably no older or ruder form of shoe known. It appears in the tombs of Egypt, and is inferior in design and execution to the Mocassin of the North American Indian. Yet it happens that there are thousands of people in Scotland who wear this shoe at this hour. It is in most common use in Shetland, but it is also frequently seen in the Orkney and Hebridean Islands. At Sand, a village quite near Lerwick, I have met a score of women wearing them, but they are to be seen all over the Shetland Islands. I am certainly within the mark when I say that thousands of pairs could at this moment be purchased in that single county." This was written in 1880, since which it is probable that the use of these shoes in the Scottish Islands has diminished.

'The only safe conclusions that can be drawn from the use of the same or a similar kind of foot-covering in ancient and modern times over so wide a field are, that necessity and opportunity taught men of different races the same primitive art, that even in so necessary and primitive an art as clothing the feet improvements often advance slowly, but once made, it becomes certain they will ultimately prevail. We can still see the *Rivelin* worn by the Shetlanders and the *Cuaran* by the Aran and St. Kilda islanders; but these survivals must before long disappear, as they have disappeared on the mainland. Yet it is curious to notice how in this, as in so many other cases, the past and obsolete custom leaves its mark in the present use, as if in small as well as great things the continuity of history must be preserved by symbols, even when the links of the chain disappear. The holes pierced in the upper part of the *Cuaran* descended to the *Brogue,* and the vandycked *fraochan* or toe-cap of the brogue may still be noticed in our nineteenth-century boots and shoes.

'DEAR SHERIFF MACKAY,—I do not now remember what I said on shoes in the discussion following your paper before the Society of Antiquaries. I will, however, jot down what occurs to me.

'If meagre and unsatisfactory in modern science and art, Gaelic is copious and descriptive in natural objects, and in the arts and sciences known to the old people. The following names for shoes will show that the people who originated them were accurate observers.

'I wish I had time to extend the list, and to avail myself more of the privilege which you have accorded me in writing these notes.—Yours very faithfully, ALEXANDER CARMICHAEL.

'7 ST. BERNARD'S ROW,
'EDINBURGH, 22nd June 1894.

'*Bachaill, brachaill, sprachaill.*—These forms are used in different localities, and mean shoes, old shoes, shapeless shoes.

'An old man in Lismore met some friends with whom he remained. When he came home his wife reproved him for drinking. He was a man of great honesty and simplicity of character, and replied, "An ta gu dearbh air m' fhalluinn fhein, a Mhor, na'n robh agamsa da bhachall bhroige dh-fhag mi nochd fhein, thu—cha 'n fheirinn aon oiche eile leat." "Indeed, and of a verity, by mine own mantle, Marion, if I had two bachalls of shoes, I would leave thee this very night; I would not remain another night with thee." The two old people were so touchingly attached to one another that they could not live apart even for a few hours.

'*Brog.*—Shoe; sock, socket; busk, busket, buskin. Brog is a generic term for socket, or that which resembles a socket; as, *brog crainn*, the socket of the mast, the step in which the mast of a boat stands; *brog na cuthaig*, shoe of the cuckoo, the blue violet; *brogach, brog-eich*, horseshoe; and *brog an eich*, shoe of the horse, coltsfoot, tussilago. The better-known name is *gullan*, while *brogach, brog an eich* is applied, and more correctly, to the leaf of the white water-lily *Nymphæa alba*. *Brog bioraich*, coltsfoot; *brog searraich*, foalsfoot, are applied to the leaf of this beautiful lily, which covers the face of some of the lakes in the Western Isles.

'*Brogan dannsaidh.*—Dancing-shoes, pumps.

'*Brogan cluaisean, brogan cluaiseanach.*—Eared shoes, shoes with flaps akin to the "Lorne shoes." *Brogan cluaisean*, eared shoes, are mentioned in old Gaelic songs.

'*Brogan cluaisean.*—Eared shoes were specially adapted for buckles, though some preferred latchets.

'In the burlesque of "Biodag air Mac-Thomais," the satirist says—

> "Tha buccallan na bhrogan
> 'S gur math gum foghnadh iall da."

> "There are buckles in his shoes
> When well the whang might do him."

'*Brog eill.*—A shoe stitched together with leather cord instead of with hemp cord. The best cord for this purpose was obtained from the seal, as was also the best leather for shoes, horse-harness, ropes, and other purposes.

'Hence the seal is spoken of among the Isles as *ron eill, ron eilleach* thong seal, thonged seal. The term occurs in many songs.

'*Brogan Gaidhealach.*—Highland shoes, known to the trade as "brogues." Shooting shoes are in imitation of these.

'*Brogan ard.*—High shoes. The toes of these high shoes, turned up as high as the ankle, sometimes as high as the middle of the leg, and occasionally as high as the knee. They were held up by cords or chains fastened to the waist, and must have been grotesque, not to say inconvenient.

'These high shoes were worn at Court, and on state occasions, in the

L

Middle Ages, and resembled those worn now by mandarins and other state-officers in China.

'The *brogan ard*, high shoes, are mentioned in the Mackintosh Lament, recovered by me in the Island of Barra.

'*Brogan direach.*—Straight shoes. The straight shoes were on alternate feet on alternate days. They were common in the Lowlands as well as in the Highlands, and down to recent times. Lord Cockburn mentions them in his *Life and Times*, and says that he wore them when he attended the High School of Edinburgh.

'*Brogan cama, cama bhrogan.*—Shaped shoes. These were shaped to the feet, and the reverse of the straight shoes.

'*Caiseart.*—Shoes, shoes of any kind. Literally, foot furnishing ; from *cas*, foot, and *beart*, furnishing.

'*Cuaran.*—Sock, socket, busk, busket, buskin, an envelope, a cover ; from *cuar*, a cover.

'The *cuaran* covers the sole, toe, heel, and sides, but not always the instep of the foot. It is laced, sometimes fancifully interlaced, over the instep.

'The *cuaran* is generally made of raw hide, preferably warm from the animal, the hide being then soft and pliable, and easily adapted to the foot. The hide over the knee was much sought after for *cuarans*, especially that over the hough. The heel of the foot fitted into the hollow of the knee, especially into the hollow of the hough, while the friction to which the knees were subjected in the lying down and the rising up of the animal rendered the skin of the knees peculiarly tough and durable.

'The *cuaran*, like the *mogais*, is made of raw hide, the hair side out, the flesh side in. In St. Kilda it is made of bird skin, the down and feathers of the bird being next the foot. The *cuaran* of the Highlands is the *pampootie* of Ireland and the *revelin* of Shetland.

'The *cuaran* is mentioned in the songs and proverbs of the people, as—

> "Must the man of the *cuarans*
> Rise an hour before the man of the shoes."

'The accepted interpretation of this doubtful proverb is that, as the wearer of *cuarans* had more lacing to do, he had to begin earlier than the wearer of shoes, who had less lacing to do.

'Probably, however, the meaning is more philosophical and far-reaching than this, implying that the poor man of the *cuarans* had to rise earlier than the rich man of the shoes.

> "He that would thrive must rise by five ;
> He that has thriven may lie till seven."

'Another proverb would seem to support this interpretation—

> "Am brogach beag, an cuaranach mor."

> "The shoey little, the cuarany big."

'Shoes were expensive, and he who indulged in them young was under the necessity when old to be content with *cuarans*. Down to recent times,

71. LORD ARCHIBALD CAMPBELL'S PIPE BAND

many children in the Highlands wore no shoes, or foot-gear of any kind. Even grown-up lads went about without shoes, often without bonnets—*ceann-ruisgte, cas-ruisgte*, head-bare, foot-bare.   Many old men in my time wore no foot-gear except on Sunday, feast-day, or some other gala-day.

'I have often seen in the Outer Isles old men and women working at their crofts barefooted, bareheaded.   Their neighbours thought none the less of them for this, nor did I.   I knew that this arose partly from habit and partly from a frugal desire to "owe no man anything," and that no head-gear or foot-gear could add to the native courtesy of mind or to the native kindliness of heart within.   On these occasions, on my deprecating any apologies for their appearance, the people would reply—

> "Ge nach duine an t-aodach,
>   Cha duine duine as aonais."

> "Though the clothing is not the man,
>   The man is not a man without it."

'A messenger came to Tongue House from Dunrobin Castle, and being a messenger of consequence, he placed his *cuarans* on the dresser.   The cook was indignant, but like a wise woman held her counsel.   When the man asked for his *cuarans* to resume his return journey, with characteristic privilege the cook asked him how he liked his breakfast.   "I never enjoyed breakfast better," replied the man.   "Then," said the cook, "you have the satisfaction of knowing that you carry your *cuarans* inside, not outside you this time.   And never you again take upon yourself to place your upstart Gower *cuarans* on the dresser of gentle folks."

'Captain Burt, in his *Letters from the North* (Letter 22), thus refers to the *Cuarans*, or "Quarants," as he terms them : "Short Stockings and *Brogues* or pumps without heels.   By the way, they cut holes in their *brogues*, though new made, to let out the water, when they have so far to go and rivers to pass ; this they do to preserve their feet from galling. . . . Some I have seen shod with a kind of pumps made out of a raw cowhide, with the hair turned outward, which, being ill made, the wearer's feet looked something like those of a rough-footed hen or pigeon.   These are called *Quarants*, and are not only offensive to the sight but intolerable to the smell of those who are near them."

'*Logais, logaisean.*—Shoes, old shoes, splayed shoes, shoes of any kind, feet, human feet, animal feet ; hence the leaf of the white water-lily is called *logais*, from its resemblance to the round, beautiful hoof of the foal.   The name occurs in an old song of Skye called "Mo roghainn 's mo run."

'Mr. John Whyte informs me that an old woman from Islay told him that she was present at the birth of a child, when she and those in charge on the occasion continued for several nights to burn *logaisean*, old shoes, to keep away the fairy folks !

'On these occasions the doors, windows, and crevices are closed, nothing being left open but the *farlos*, in the ridge of the roof, for the egress of smoke and the ingress of light.   The smell of burning leather filling the house, and escaping through the *farlos*, keeps the fairy folks from entering and spiriting away either mother or child.   Iron pins and spikes are driven into the ground and wall round the mother and child, to safeguard them till the baptism of the one and the purification of the other.   When the child and mother have gone under the hands of the *pears eaglais*, *persona ecclesia*, they are safe, and the pins are removed.

'There is no increase on the women of fairyland, hence the desire to spirit away children, and mothers to nurse them.   Innumerable stories, in prose and rhyme, graphic and realistic, are told throughout the Highlands and Islands of newly-born babes and of parturient women carried away to the *bruthainn shìth nan sìthichean*, underground bowers of the fairies.

'*Mogais*, plural *mogaisean* (Anglicised, *moggins*, or *muggins*, *moggasheens*, or *muggasheens*).—Shoes, ankle-shoes, shoes coming up the calf of the leg. It is singular that in name, as in appearance, the *mogaisean* of the High-landers should be identical with the *moccasins* of the Red Indians.   Possibly the writer who introduced the name of the foot-gear of the Indians was a Highlander, accustomed to the name of the similar foot-gear of his country-men.

'*Mogais* holds the same relation to the *cuaran* that the boot does to the shoe.   The word is from *mog*, a husk, a sheath, a cylinder, and occurs in various forms, as *mogal peasair*, pease husk ; *mogal ponair*, bean husk ; *mogan*, a footless stocking ; *mogan brigis*, leg of a trouser.

'*Slaopag*.—This term for an old shapeless shoe, which is not to be found in dictionaries of Modern Gaelic, occurs in a lullaby, which I got at Bunawe, along with several other archaic words.'

72. THE CUP OF MACIAN OF GLENCOE

CHAPTER XIII

MISCELLANEOUS

MACIAN'S CUP

Sir Duncan Campbell of Barcaldine was kind enough
to give the writer a photograph of the silver cup which
tradition says belonged to MacIan of Glencoe, and is
the property of Captain Duncan Cameron MacDonald
of Glencoe, Argyll and Bute Artillery Militia, late Her
Majesty's Deputy Commissioner and Vice-Consul, Oil
River Protectorate.

Mrs. Ballingall, the sister of this gentleman, gives the
following account of the cup :—

'I do not know any story attached to the cup before the
Massacre of Glencoe, but as it is said to be an old French cup
of the sixteenth century, I have no doubt it was brought to
Glencoe by old MacIan when he came back from Paris in his
youth. The story of it is, but of course from oral tradition
only, that MacIan drank out of it and pledged his foes the
night before the massacre, and that afterwards when the surviv-
ing MacDonalds came back they found it in the ruins of the
house among the ashes on the hearth.'

Mrs. Ballingall, *née* Ellen MacDonald, in a letter to
Sir Duncan Campbell, says :—

'As far as I am concerned, and I am sure I may speak for

the rest of my family, Lord Archibald Campbell is at perfect liberty to make what use he chooses of the photograph of MacIan's cup; and for myself, I may add I am very pleased it should be in Lord Archibald's book.'

THE BELL OF ST. FILLAN AT KILLIN.

In September 1882 the late Charles Stewart of Killin showed the writer the Celtic bell which is called St. Fillan's bell.   It hung formerly in the old chapel at Killin.   He asked the writer if he had seen it, and went to fetch it.   Having re-entered the room, he placed the bell on a low ottoman seat in the bay-window of his sitting-room ; the sun was streaming in, and the light fell strongly on the old bell, which, though greatly worn, was covered with the remains of Celtic interwoven knots and patterns.   Mr. Stewart had gone out of the room to fetch some weapons, and on his return the writer asked him if he had ever noticed any patterns on the bell. He replied he had not, and what was more, it had gone up to Edinburgh and had been seen by all the *savants* there, who had noted no such characteristic about the bell ; he, however, at once saw the patterns.   A little later on in the year the writer visited the Antiquarian Museum, which was then in the building on the Mound, Edinburgh, since which date the fine collection has found a new home in Queen Street, Edinburgh.   It was here that the discovery made at Killin received confirmation, for several other bells showed the beautiful Celtic knotted patterns observed in the bell at Killin.

It is a curious fact that some fail to see the remains of this ornamentation. Strong sunlight, or perhaps electric light, will reveal this hidden beauty. The work was in all probability what is termed *niello* work by the Italians. When the secret of this art was first known to and practised by the Celts is likely to remain uncertain, but it must date from very ancient days. The style of art is the same as that observable in the early Irish and Scottish manuscripts.

INDEX

Printed by T. and A. CONSTABLE, Printers to Her Majesty
at the Edinburgh University Press